adrienne
maree brown

ANCESTORS

BLACK DAWN SERIES

With the Black Dawn series we honor anarchist traditions and follow the great Octavia E. Butler's legacy. Black Dawn seeks to explore themes that do not reinforce dependency on oppressive forces (the state, police, capitalism, elected officials) and will generally express the values of antiracism, feminism, anticolonialism, and anticapitalism. With its natural creation of alternate universes and world-building, speculative fiction acts as a perfect tool for imagining how to bring forth a just and free world. The stories published here center queerness, Blackness, antifascism, and celebrate voices previously disenfranchised, all who are essential in establishing a society in which no one is oppressed or exploited. Welcome, friends, to Black Dawn!

BLACK DAWN SERIES #6

SANINA L. CLARK, SERIES EDITOR

Copyright 2025 by adrienne maree brown, LLC
This edition copyright 2025, AK Press (Chico / Edinburgh)
ISBN 9781849355520
E-ISBN 9781849355537
LCCN: 2024949071

AK Press	AK Press
370 Ryan Ave. #100	33 Tower Street
Chico, CA 95973	Edinburgh, Scotland EH6 7BN
www.akpress.org	akuk.com

"Listening/Honor Song" by John Trudell/Milton Sahme © 1983 Poet Tree Publishing/Quilt Man Music
"The Spoken Forest" by Ernestine Hayes reprinted by permission of the writer.

Cover art by Juan Carlos Barquet, www.jcbarquet.com
Illustrations by Juna Clark
Cover design and logo by T. L. Simons, tlsimons.com
Printed in the USA

This final installment of the Grievers Trilogy is dedicated to Charity, Blair, Grace, Sheddy, Ron, Mama Lila, Mama Sandra, General Baker, the infant phenomenon, and the lost one. This trilogy is a love note to every people who have survived genocide and extinction, and a lit candle for the peoples, species, and cultures we have already lost.

Rest in pleasure, rest in possibility.

ANCESTORS

Dune's Maps

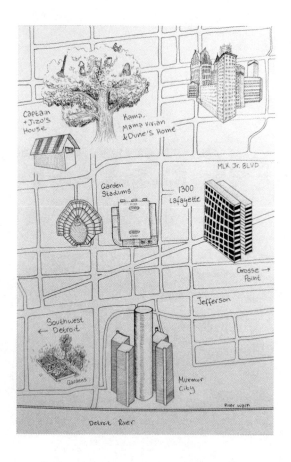

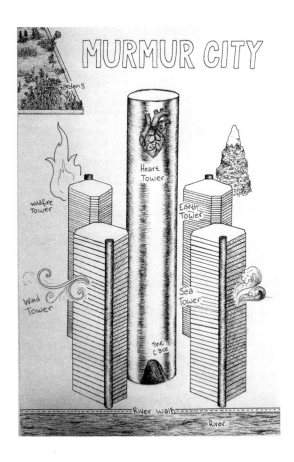

The Spoken Forest

I was thinking about the forest one day
and it came to me—
our stories,
our songs,
our names,
our history,
our memories
are not lost.

All these riches are being kept for us
by our aunties, our uncles,
our grandparents, our relatives—
those namesakes who walk and dance
wearing robes that make them seem like bears
and wolves

Our loved ones.
Those beings who live in the spoken forest.
They are holding everything for us.

    —Ernestine Hayes

"Wage love!"
— Charity Mahouna Hicks

Prologue

Even when it all seems to be falling apart, something deeper down is busy mending. After the storm washes one world away, be astounded—look how many creatures are already building the next world in the rubble and mud, persistent. This is who we are, time workers. As long as there is a pulse between us, there are many places to grow, and many lives to live. When there appears to be no way out, we grow wild inside ourselves, into the infinite interior.

Detroit had been a city of beauty and corruption, ubiquitous Blackness and post-capitalist solution. Now, Detroit has become a land of grief and possibility, of risk and absence—a fertile soil thick with spiritual hunger and people determined to live against all odds.

Less than a thousand people are left in the city after the H-8 virus lifted generations of Black souls out of their bodies and scared everyone else into evacuation. Three years into their survival, most of them have moved into Murmur City, once known as the General Motors Renaissance Center, on the Detroit River. A community of Anishinaabe and other Indigenous survivors are making an old new way in the middle of the river, on an island they know well. Other survivors still run wild. They are all protected, or contained, by an impenetrable wall of vines and lush leaves sprouted from magic. The wilderness has become the norm.

Dune's Ancestor Journal, June

haven't you wondered who has been telling you this story? who knows the names of each person, who can trace their tales back through time? who was right there when dune dragged a dead mother through the house, sang to a dying grandmother, survived a pandemic, lost herself, brought home a stray dog, then a stray gay, then a grandfather and a child, and then made a little utopian prison for everyone she knows? who can almost see dune now, almost feel her?

it is me, kama.

i am very much the fuck here, just here, shamelessly bound to my child. all of us here are bound to the living, and all of us tell the story of the living, through whatever portals will open. i have been blessed with the story of this fugitive, beloved, maroon detroit, where we are free. yes, we—we are thick with freedom when freedom is what our descendants know. as long as our species lives, its ancestors live in the spirit realm. when the species is extinct, no longer remembered by its own kind because every creature who held such a memory has died, the spirits are released back into the wild and great energy of all life.

the individual of everything is the everything of existence.

responsibility is not a universal assumption. we don't have to pay attention. many ancestors don't, many of them rest, many of them cluster into common or co-supportive narratives of what we are: heaven cluster, nirvana cluster, purgatory cluster, nothingness cluster, bardo cluster, and so on. each visually distinct, though i can never decide which aspect of their looks expresses their uniformity. some of those clusters explore their connection to their successors, some don't. my cluster is full of interventionists, retired organizers, and busybodies. we partner with the living through stories.

you think it's dune you love, but it's me. i am the storyteller. i am an architect of survival for my people and my child. i am a warrior queen.

and i'm a fucking ghost! i'm furious about that. so are a lot of the ancestors who were initiated into spirit before our times. there is a correct moment of initiation for each person, just as there is a right time to live a bodylife. when we show up early to this afterlife it literally fucks up the world.

we have to manage the crowd, so sometimes we have to share a bodylife. that shit sucks for everyone involved.

did you notice that dune fell in love with a man like me? always talking so loud, but secretive, hard to know. passionate, but un-tie-downable. can survive amongst the whites, can properly bed down a black girl who don't like boys. tuh. but my daughter knows love and pleasure and that makes all of us so happy because pleasure is the shiver of god available in a lifetime.

i love your surprise, how you are telling yourself you knew i was with you all along and the whole time. i can feel your curiosity about how much i'm going to tell you about the world beyond death. everything. nothing. you'll believe the wrong amount, too much, or not enough anyway. humans are always off the mark by some measure.

i is for the living. it's quite difficult speaking in the i as a spirit. it's crowded; i have to let my story flow down a river full of stories. we're going to rest. my story is as real as the inner one you're always telling yourself about your own life. we will tell as much as we can.

Dune sat back, setting her pen down and shaking out her hand. She was half awake; these thoughts, which she heard in her dead mother Kama's voice, had pulled her from bed to desk, from dreaming to scribbling. Now, she was immediately exhausted again. She closed the notebook, confused, and shuffled back down the hall, climbing into the bed, scooting back against Dawud for warmth.

Part I

Summer, Keep Turning

Summer in Murmur City

Ghosts

Every place Dune went now was thick; the air full and pushing up against her, each room crowded with something more than bodies. She was learning to breathe with ghosts, through ghosts—to breathe in the dead. Each surface held silhouettes and stills, half faces in the stucco, in the bathroom floor tile, in the carpet piling, the laundry lint, the swept dirt. Figures emerged in the tree bark, the lone wave, the cloud cover. Still shots from another realm. The shadows at her periphery took forms, impossible to look at directly, but always there, and always watching her.

In the hottest stretch of a Detroit summer, the sun made the sidewalks sizzle, made everything blur at the edges, steaming and wavering as the world blazed and cooked.

For the first time, Dune thought that maybe no one had ever left the Earth. That every single life, once lived, became part of the material of the made world. That she had been naive, not seeing it all until now. But maybe she just needed to get out of the sun.

She wondered how everyone else was going through life, swimming in all this spirit but not seeming to feel or see the presence, the pressure.

Orphan

When most people in Murmur City saw Dune, what they really saw was the absence of Kama all around her. They'd all experienced cataclysmic loss, but Kama belonged to the community as much as she had ever belonged to her child. Dune had been the shy addendum to Kama's presence, an old-soul baby passed around at food co-op meetings. Then, a quiet, observant kid, set in the corner with her homework as the community strategized resistance to the gentrification of the Detroit they had sustained through economic devastation. As they missed Kama, they looked for traces of her big laugh and grounded leadership to emerge in this sullen, private, dazed, magical young adult.

Dune could feel the unspoken condolences, the desire people had to connect themselves to her through her dead mother. She wondered how long this would last, knowing that for some people, it's the rest of their lives, that people will say, "Oh, her mother died too soon, that's why she is unfinished." And others will lower their shaking heads, saying no to such a world, thinking of their own imperfect mothers.

Marta

June 22

Dear Dune,

I know you're in there. I don't know if you're alive, but if you have made it this long, I know you are somewhere behind that green cage around Detroit. I don't know if this will reach you. Like, is there internet in there?

I'm still in Miami. My grandma died, last September, old age. I got to be with her, basically took care of her those last few months. My mom like couldn't handle it, couldn't watch her die. Which it's not like I *could* watch her die, but someone had to be there, so I was. I feel a bit desperate to show you I am redeemable.

Anyway, long story short, I'm sorry about what I said about Mama Vivian before I left. I'm sorry about a lot of things. I been thinking about you a lot, about what you said about how selfish I was. I wanted to bring you with me, and I didn't really think through what that would mean for you.

I hope you forgive me, wherever you are.

Are you in Detroit?

Are there people in there?

With love forever,

Marta

Dog

Dog had not endorsed the move into Murmur City—he didn't like the smell of the place, or being reliant on humans for going outside.

Dune had worked with Hoka and the security team to come up with a solution, a rolling service door on the street level that was left open just a foot. A human would have a hard time sneaking in, but Dog could easily scoot under and make his way through the gut of the building into the atrium. The security system let surveillance know when anyone entered or left the structure, so they learned Dog's schedule. Dog knew how to find Dune and Dawud's tower, and everyone else knew to push Dune's floor in the elevator when Dog arrived. Dog could reach the elevator down button.

Dawud and Dune had worked together to make a doggy door in their unit and turned one of the empty offices on their floor into a space just for Dog, with a room that served as an indoor bathroom area. Dawud had found a sex dungeon in Corktown with all these squirt friendly washable rugs and blankets, some of which they repurposed to create a place where Dog could pee. The creature never did more than that indoors—even during the frozen months, he shat outside—and Dune understood.

Dog still had as many names as he had friends. To truly know someone in Murmur City was to know their name, their pronouns, which tower they called home, and their name for this dog of the people. In Dune's household, Dog was called Dog, Rudy, Delilah-Must-Have-Sent-You, and a rapid chest thump that Jizo did in honor of Dog's tail in moments of joy or anticipation.

Dog could go anywhere he wanted, anytime. But even now, peak of summer, this was where he wanted to be, resting at Dune's feet, free, choosing her.

Captain

Captain had landed in Murmur City victorious. He had served his last mission; he had gotten himself and Jizo across one last battlefield. He sat in their quarters in a chair facing the city and talked to Delilah. Not about her, not of her. He had lengthy, complex conversations *with her*, remembering their lives together and processing whatever Dune and Dawud told him was happening in the community.

More and more often, he didn't speak to whoever was there with him, choosing to stay in dialogue with Delilah, flirting and gesturing with the ghost sitting on his left. Dune felt she was working with Delilah now, in an unspoken collaboration to give Captain a soft transition.

Over their first six months in Murmur City, Captain had slowly, one request at a time, organized the furniture in his and Jizo's quarters so that it felt like home. He'd had them turn the furniture away from the wall-mounted TV and toward the window full of city. He'd had the small table pulled into the center of the open space. He'd sent Dawud on missions to gather the art from his place, curling and faded images of painted Black people living their lives, photos of friends and family long dead. As each piece had fallen into place he would calm, stop pointing and gesturing, letting his hands rest, curled and stiff, in his lap.

After a few dinners in the atrium, Dune had realized how overwhelming it was for Captain, wheeling there and back, being peppered with questions about what he wanted to eat and drink, and well-meaning attempts by strangers to get to know him. All with Delilah there and God forbid if people ignored her. He had a public setting and would launch into storytelling, sometimes delightful, sometimes offensive, always loud. It took so much out of him.

When Dune offered to bring a meal to the room for him, his open relief was clear guidance. After that, she took turns with Dawud and Jizo, bringing dinner to Captain and sitting with him, sometimes bringing along one of the handful of people he seemed to like.

It was enough.

Dawud

"Verily I say unto you, what in matter of fact is up though? Ha, naw, I'm just play-play, whatupdoe Dirty D, Detroit City? It's a scorching, disgusting summer day so BLAST those air conditioners and do not let the heat win—this is your annual, seasonal, monthly, weekly, and daily reminder to keep it cool and keep it hydrated if you want to keep it smooth and pretty like Daddy's perfect calves. And that reminder is highlighted on the page for my pale-skinned brethrenitos and brethrenettes: don't get dry and dusty and lonely and crusty. But most of all don't get musty cause the windows do not open in this crystal dungeon. A wise man once said, 'time keeps on slipping into the future,' and here today to discuss the whimsical flimsy of time is my dear friend and creative comrade, the elusive Master of the Wall, Dune Chen."

Dune cut her eyes at Dawud across the studio. She was reading, trying to mind her business while he laid down some intros for episodes he'd already recorded. "Once again our brilliant warden will be giving a silent interview while I pull a fantastical world from my sacred anus."

Dune lit a spliff, rolled with tobacco and weed grown just a few miles from her old home. Dawud continued, "Oh, how am *I*? You beautiful sexy little sloth, I thought you would literally never ever ask. I'm doing ok, you know there is so much to do every day that it amazes me I do not have a boss, which means I am creating this condition, abusing my power against myself. Every day I shock and manipulate myself out of bed, tease myself with a near breakfast experience while I long for pork-fat sizzling bacon, jumbo cage-free eggs, and some kind of stinky French queso. I walk around as a self-appointed journalist, listening between the lines to what's happening all over this beautiful city, so that I can come through these doors and zeitgeist my way through your wants all the way deep into your needs. Right now you need me to tell you, *you are not crazy*—it's getting a little bit the-same-every-fucking-day in here and I'll just say it, we need more entertainers. I cannot keep carrying this entire population on my fine ass and beautiful brain."

This got a laugh from Dune, so he doubled down. "And I rarely, rarely spend any time talking about what a catch I am, but I look so delicious every day without trying, I am the smartest man in three towers, I'm obviously hilarious, and I'm incredible in bed. Black don't crack. And I am gay (still) so if you are gay, please check yes, right there in the little box on my heart."

Dune shook her head. When Dawud finished, she poked him. "You need to help me find the lesbians too, then, if it's hoe season."

"It's always hoe season in southern California. You have Rio. I need a cute booty blaster, asap."

"I *don't* have Rio."

"You would if you could and you could if you would. You actually have something even better—a fucking romance novel."

"I can't tell if you're joking, Dawud."

"Me neither."

Rio

"So Chene Park is officially your favorite spot?" Rio sat next to Sahari on the stage of the famous amphitheater that gleamed white like a Mormon temple on the south bank of the Detroit River.

"I mean . . . first of all, it's the Aretha Franklin Amphitheater now," Sahari held a professorial finger in the air. "Right here where we currently sit, Aretha herself, and Erykah Badu and India Arie, and Stevie Wonder and Chaka Khan, all performed! Mary J. Blige stomped right there."

"And that's what you love? The proximity to fame?" Rio asked, deadpan. Sahari noticed again just how beautiful Rio was to look at, their eyes always a bit suspicious, their arms strong and relaxed, holding her hips as they often did when they sat this close, legs intertwined.

"It feels like we've spent an eternity, now, living inside this hedge, this cage. Can there be a favorite spot in a prison? I like to write here. Here and Heidelberg Project, but it feels weirder and weirder to go there, like nature was collaborating with the art houses, but now it's reclaiming everything. But this place, being in here feels like freedom some days, like before. When the waves of claustrophobia wash over me I come here, walk over there and lie down and just look straight up at the sky, through clouds and atmosphere all the way to eternal space."

Sahari stayed at the intersection of gratitude and growling about the conditions. She wrapped her long black locs around her hand a few times, absentminded.

"You wanted to talk?" Rio brought Sahari back to the moment. Sahari's black skin caught light from a different galaxy, Rio was convinced. Sahari's eyes were wide, for a moment she looked terrified to find herself in the present.

"Yes." Sahari closed her eyes, gathered herself. "Actually, I want to read you something. I just need you to hear it, so we can be authentic about all of this."

Rio nodded consent. Sahari rolled back and grabbed her bag, leather that had been carved and stained into a prayer. She pulled a journal out of it that was thick, well-used, and looked too full to find anything in. She easily turned to a page about three-quarters into the book, and looked up briefly to make sure Rio was . . . Still there? Paying attention? "Ok."

I picked a lover at this end of the world, thinking I knew who was left in my life. Rio was my choice. Of the seven hundred souls here, yes, and if there were seven billion others within this oasis for the dead, I still would have found Rio, and done anything to be with them.

We weren't exclusive, I knew better than to try that move. Rio is at their best and happiest when they feel free. I hoped it was an unnecessary conversation. Dune and her wall of weeds were unexpected. We can't leave, you got a man, and you still want mine? I didn't want to share. I don't want to share. Casual was one thing, but Rio thinks they love her . . . Some days I feel like all I can do is delay the inevitable.

Sahari didn't look up to see how this was landing on Rio, so she missed the surprise, the sweetness, and the shame that flashed across Rio's cheeks and eyes. Rio was grateful for the privacy.

They aren't sleeping together now, but they might as well be. The energy I want to be focused on me, the energy I remember when I was the light in Rio's eye—that energy has split. Even when Rio is with me, holding me, inside of me, I can feel that part of them is now with Dune. My heart has been breaking slowly and I know that a moment will come when I have to stop pretending like Rio has chosen me, when really they are just trying to protect my heart.

The world seems impossibly small now. I cannot imagine who else would ever move me the way Rio does. I ride the circle of the city, feeling nauseous with future heartache, trying to feel it enough to release it, to not bring it home and rush the ending with stupid fights over things Rio can't control. I try to just bring sweetness home to offer my lover, certain they want a different taste altogether.

When Rio leaves me, I don't know what I will do. I don't know if I can handle it. I'll be alone. I can tell myself that everyone I lost to H-8 wanted to be with me, were taken from me. But Rio? Rio feels like the love of my life and they're rejecting me. How do they not know yet that I'm their person? And Dune is just a cool prison warden.

I'm scared of the worst, that they just don't feel the way I do. This thought makes me cry so hard that I feel like I'm having an emotional affair with myself, cleaning up the mess before I see Rio again. They are so kind to me now, so attentive, but something in it feels like a lie, like they are fulfilling an obligation I never asked for. I just want to be loved, to be chosen. By Rio. And now I don't know how to tell Rio what they actually mean to me—they'll think it's manipulation. Maybe it's not even love now, just escalating terror, swallowed.

Sahari went quiet, closing her eyes and breathing in and out heavily. She had walked a mountain, getting this message across the space between them. Tears quietly spilled from her closed eyes, fast, dripping down her chin.

Rio reached up and cupped Sahari's face with both hands, catching the tears, using their thumbs to brush more sea from her cheeks. In the years of their relationship, Rio had learned of Sahari's history of substance abuse and really chaotic relationships and suicidal ideation. Sahari had been staying at the shelter on Mac when H-8 hit, her ex had put her out after cheating on her. She almost died by suicide a month before the virus came, and twice before that. Her fragile hold on life made those close to her want to protect her, and Rio was not immune. They wanted to support her in this moment without becoming a trigger. For a while they were still together, holding the release of something so big it could break them. It could mean they were already broken.

"How do you feel now that you read it to me?"

Sahari's eyes popped open, surprised by the question. "Um . . . good. Scared by what comes after this, but I can feel my jaw relaxing, my shoulders soften."

Rio nodded. "Ok if I respond a bit now, and then maybe sleep on it too?"

Sahari smiled, grateful as always for the way Rio slowed everything down. Rio was trying to cut through the loops Sahari could get lost in.

"I love you, Sahari. I am so proud of you sharing this with me, telling me about it instead of running off and shit."

They shared a look. When Sahari ran, it was often towards a debilitating high, and sometimes towards dangerous depressive episodes.

"I'm here with you because I chose to be a family with you, because you are kind, you are steady, you are brilliant, you are sexy, you are incredible, you are fun, you do what you say you are going to do. And like you said, we *weren't* exclusive. Neither of us. Being the lesser hoe in our loveship doesn't make you monogamous." They both let the moment be flirtatious, piling up the soft landing.

"When we were deciding to do this, all we knew was that we loved fucking each other and we didn't fight over stupid shit. And everyone was dying, and we were probably going to die too, but shit, since we're here let's hold on to each other. We didn't have any kind of usual romantic process. When you say I don't feel the same way, I'm like, I don't know how you feel. I don't think you know how I feel. And even for me, I have been a hoe and I have been non-monogamous, but I don't know if I have ever been polyamorous for real, felt love for more than one person at the same time. Love has kept me honest about how I felt. Love has helped me hold your boundary without much argument. But do I wish, hope, we figure something out eventually that . . . allows us both to be ourselves? I do. And I'm in no rush. We here, we safe, I'm good."

Sahari looked up once Rio stopped talking, lashes clumped by her pain.

"Is that enough for you, Rio?"

"This feels like a crazy question to me, babe. Not that you're crazy, but that you're asking me to make a crazy statement." Rio bit their lip. "I'm saying that I feel love for you *and* love for Dune. And I understand that you're not comfortable with me exploring all that right now, and I'm ok with that, I'm ok with staying right here and building this good life together. *And* I hope it changes with time, if you get to know her . . ."

"No, Rio. I don't need to know more about her. She controls my life, and I didn't give her permission to. She already has someone. She has everything!" Sahari caught herself getting loud.

Rio kept their hands on Sahari, trying to stay connected. "I'm sorry. I never bring this up because I don't think anything has changed. But you brought me here today to tell me that what I am doing is not enough. Holding the boundary is not enough . . . Is that the thing you most need me to hear?"

Sahari nodded yes, eyes raw. "I'm sorry. I don't want to be like this. But I don't think I can do this if you love her. Even if you spend your days and nights with me. I want all of you."

"Or none?" Rio looked deeply hurt asking this.

Sahari looked away. "I don't want to feel ashamed about this,

Rio. I am not the first person to want romantic monogamy. I am not crazy."

"Nobody is crazy here, not for that reason. For staying in Detroit, yes. But not for loving the way we love." Rio reached over and pulled Sahari in closer, until they were in each other's laps. They kissed her forehead, her crying eyes, her damp cheeks, her slurring mouth. Sahari cried harder and uglier, rough groaning tears. Rio kept kissing her, receiving it all.

That was enough. For now.

Jizo

Jizo was about half magic–half boy these days. On the boy days, he went to school, he had friends. He charmed every soul in Murmur City, remixed his hand-me-down wardrobe into fashion, and was a beloved member of the community. On the magic days, he might disappear, gone from his and Captain's apartment before the sun rose, returning in the evening, full of stories he couldn't tell because there were no words for where he'd been and what he had experienced.

The school was in the old Learning Center, a series of modern classrooms on the first floor. About one in four humans in Murmur City was under the age of eighteen, and the school was designed as a free learning space where kids were self-guided and could teach each other. The adults were there to help, to make sure kids were safe and accounted for. The school offered life-skills sessions for each age group, and had distinct cross-age cohorts. There was so much space and encouragement for each person to be themselves. Only a handful of people had graduated so far, but the practice beyond school was a period of apprenticeship where young adults could try on different kinds of work that was needed in the community, to see where they could best contribute.

Jizo had connected with the deaf elementary community in Murmur City and was learning ASL, as was most of his little family. Captain didn't mess with "that ASL" cause, "we understand each other just fine, y'all just don't know how to listen."

On boy days, Jizo dazzled them with poetic stories that moved through his entire body, language like a dance. On magic days, he forgot what he had learned and communicated in his special Jizo way, which was just as clear to them as a spirit boy could be.

He was learning a ton, both in terms of how to communicate, and the norms of this unfolding society. Physically, he had changed very little in his time at Murmur City. His body was in a holding pattern that seemed directly related to Captain, who loved having a perpetual grandson and didn't have that much time left. So Jizo was a boy with enough magic to stay a boy.

A lot of people in Murmur City had had magic, though much of it was fading as the dangers of the world beyond the wall slipped into the past. Most of the magic was related to what they could see, what they could hear, what they could feel. Most of the magic was a radical shift of awareness around where memories were held, and how much any one thing influenced everything else. Most of the magic was an emergence of ways of listening beyond the surface of the material world because they were in a place where the spirits greatly outnumbered the bodies.

Because it had emerged during a time of duress, magic now barely registered; in the world before, everyone would have been daunted by a mystery like Jizo. But in Murmur City, everything was reshaped by disaster and magic, and Jizo was just another surviving delight.

Ghosts vs Spirits

Dune's Ancestor Journal, June
ghosts haunt a person. spirits haunt a place.
haunt *is too big a word, when you have no material impact; linger is more appropriate. we linger, overlapping each other in rustling winds, paper soft enough to tear if it could be touched. my sense of self is rare. even as i speak to you, i feel a million voices sliding against me, wanting the channel. mostly i feel multitudinous, moving in relationship to others, all of our longings fluttering into direction. more and less present. more and less memory. more and less dream. but the place matters.*

we linger in rhythms, trilling around a corner with enough rage to slightly shift the hair against the neck of our living beloved. which of us loved her? all of us; all of us loved her in every way. precious as her mother and her father, as her teacher, as her sibling, as her friend, as her pet, as the first mouth she kissed, as the first finger to slide along the inside of her belt, as her soulmate, as her deity, as her coffin, as the fire that undid her.

Mama Rue

Once a month, Mohamed did a briefing for the Mbongi Council where he updated a laminated map of occupied and used spaces in the interconnected, seven-building structure with a dry-erase marker that smelled of poisoned berries. Murmur City was a growing body inside the physical container that had long been known as the Renaissance Center, or RenCen—part hotel, part office building for General Motors, part conference center, all of the Detroit skyline. There were spaces being reclaimed and repurposed regularly. Yesterday, Mohamed mentioned that the old Summit restaurant had been converted into a quiet space in which to read or write. Opened as a spinning penthouse flex in 1977, the Summit had stopped turning at some point, been renamed a few times, and still had the best views in the state. Dune had had to talk herself down from walking right out of the meeting and going up there.

Now Dune was stepping off the elevator at the top of the Heart Tower, with two books in her satchel, and there in front of her was a beautiful hand-drawn sign for the Code Midnight Reading Room. Following the signs along a round hallway, she found what she had been looking for, waiting for, needing in its absence. The windows were floor to ceiling, the floor a pattern of hardwood that looked like diamonds and time travel. It was an astoundingly clear blue day, and light poured into the room from every direction.

Dune scanned the room for an empty table right next to the windows, wanting her solitude. A few people, familiar and strange, were spread out at the wooden tables: reading, alone and together. She started to move across the room, but then she spotted her mentor Mama Rue at the far end of the space.

Mama Rue had pulled a chair away from its table and sat at an angle, head tilted up like a cat towards the sun, facing the city, feeling the city. Dune approached slowly, at an angle that allowed her to watch the elder's face. Her eyes moved as if people watching, though when Dune followed those busy eyes out the window all she saw were empty streets.

In Murmur City, people respected Mama Rue, and Dune was learning all the reasons why. It was the respect reserved for the old and the mad, the respect that doesn't interrupt incoherence, but doesn't try to knit all the chaos into lessons either.

"Mama Rue?"

Mama Rue's eyes softened. For a moment, it looked like the very texture of her eyes blurred and shifted. Then her velvety Black face, folded in a million places by past emotion, turned towards Dune. "Yes child?"

"What are you looking at?" Dune sat.

"I wish I could show you," Mama Rue spoke clear and slow, "and I'm glad you asked. I'm looking at our people."

Dune felt a gnawing in her gut so deep it made her grip her chair to keep from disappearing. She had a sudden urge to look through Mama Rue's eyes, to take them for herself like stealing sunglasses, to look for Kama. This only felt slightly unreasonable.

"Say more?"

Mama Rue's face looked equally indulgent and concerned. "They're not gone. No one wants to believe me. But I know souls, that's my work. I used to be able to touch a soul and heal a body. Might could still do. But you can feel when a place is thick with souls. I been places where they tell me it's a beach, it's a restaurant, it's a park, but I can *feel* it was a battleground, a mass grave, a transgression. Souls leave imprints. Some haunt around briefly and then they go. But this is new. I'm very old for something new to be happening, so at first I dismissed it. But it's still happening."

"What's happening?"

"They're here. They didn't die, they're all there. I can feel them. I can feel the presence of them all the time. A city can feel full or empty, Detroit has felt both ways. It's full right now." Mama Rue's eyes turned back to the window, changing again as Dune watched, getting softer, wider, eyebrows relaxed. "It's the fullest it's ever been right now. I feel them, and sometimes I can see them. A Black and glorious city. Yes, the city has decreased in living souls! But just from evacuation, not from H-8. Those souls stayed here. They're right there. And there's more, there's others, the city is vibrant with them."

Dune hesitated and then decided there was little risk to sharing; Mama Rue was too gone for gossip. Maybe here Dune could speak freely. "I feel that too. I feel like there are people all around me all the time. I don't see them most of the time, but I feel them?"

Mama Rue nodded and moved as if she would grab Dune's wrist, but thought better of it. "Jot down what you hear, what they say, whatever you can pull from the noise. Start a journal of the dead, write it down verbatim. Let them tell their stories to you."

"Bet." Dune was a death documentarian, writing down data, facts, observations. Writing down these . . . ancestral feelings? . . . felt like a different, self-indulgent thing. But Mama Rue's homework always had purpose. Maybe what Mama Rue was saying was that these feelings were a kind of data, too? She wanted to ask Mama Rue for Kama, for Elouise, for her people. It felt equal parts too selfish and too precise. She asked, "Do you recognize anyone?"

Mama Rue laughed without turning from the window, "Of course."

Dune couldn't handle this. She wanted her mother. There is a moment between a deep cut and the beginning of the bleed, and Dune was there. Knowing Kama was here but not visible to her might be the end of Dune, might be too much. She couldn't think of a way out of the conversation. She drifted back and, when she was sure Mama Rue had gotten completely immersed in that other Detroit, Dune slipped off to the farthest table and began her own watching.

Dune's Ancestor Journal, June

we were not interested in being good. not that we wanted to be evil, or mean or anything. but being good was a path that had already been walked so many times, to such harmful ends. there was nothing original gonna happen in our lives if we spent our time trying to stay within the footsteps and grooves and fences and gates that were established to be good. we wanted something worth living, a life worth living, and we sensed that stepping out of the way of good would be part of it.

we wanted to reckon with the whole thing—we wanted to have a fucking story. we made big mistakes, and we paid the cost. we opened our hearts to people who were clearly possessed by demons. we kissed people who were obviously created to cast spells with their mouths. we let people make love to us even when their true form was showing, and we were terrified. in each instance we felt alive, and we felt affirmed that we were not, and never could be, the thing that we were touching and being touched by. we could be curious about it, we could be hurt by it, but something in us was intact and unbothered.

in that sticky forbidden pleasure, that's when we started, or maybe revisited, thinking about being good. like what if we were fundamentally good already, not because of our external actions, but because of who we were, who we are, how wonderful we could make a moment. what if there was nothing to do but love and notice ourselves and others?

Mbongi Council

The low murmuring, resting sounds of the Mbongi Council had annoyed Dune since she had become a reluctant council member. The implications of everyone having conversations they didn't want overheard always put her on edge. Dune wanted to be at the swimming hole, basking on the rock, not in this air-conditioned atrium where the sun was only a refracted suggestion. She wasn't interested in this pre-game, when people tried to move each other around the chess board of opinion. She wasn't interested in how Mbongi Council spent so much time talking. This quality time that could be used for gardening, gathering supplies, teaching, food prep, security runs, or even poetry was instead used for this politicking.

She liked a lot of these people individually. Outside of the council, Mama Tazina was a dear friend who Dune sought out for shifts in perspective. Hoka and Bineshii were elders who had been friends with her parents, with her grandmother Mama Vivian, and who now kept an eye on Dune, part friends, part mentors. Mohamed was one of the first people she'd met in Murmur City, and she deeply respected him. These were people she would want to spend time with in most contexts. Except Ed, who was an older white man who'd chosen "devil's advocate" as his life path, but showed up to every single meeting willing to do the most tedious tasks. She loved, liked, or at least respected everyone in the room. But as soon as the meeting started, a different energy emerged.

With a dramatic clearing of her throat, a small Black woman named Stacie stood up to chair this week's meeting. She meant well, but had a hyperbolic energy, a posturing of a larger, more historic self than the moment called for. Dune suspected that a lot of people on the council enjoyed this part the most, representing a lineage of thought, swaying each other.

The Mbongi Council had set up "Community Needs" boxes in the Heart Tower dining room and in the Riverview Atrium for gathering requests and feedback from the general public. Once a month, they offered open report-backs to the community about how they were responding to these needs and managing collective resources. They mostly focused on what was happening in Murmur City, but got reports on the larger trends in Maroon Detroit, too. The council's meetings were generally open if people wanted to witness or raise an issue, though it was rare for people who weren't on the council or presenting on the agenda to attend—there was work to do. The secretary, currently Hoka, went through the needs boxes and organized an agenda, and the council proceeded to discuss each topic. The issues felt repetitive to Dune. She thought they could come up with a general protocol for decision making and apply it—what's the best option for the majority of people?

But then again, knowing the council, they would have different opinions on "best," "option," "majority," and "people." Listening to the back and forth made Dune miss her father, how he used to cut through an emotional tangle with a non-negotiable piece of data that moved everything along. Like his story of buying their home: "I'll pay the appraisal price; this isn't a matter of opinion or our feelings on worth." So much of the content of these meetings were rehashing opinions on things that weren't a matter of opinion. So here they sat, every week, for a full day, discussing whichever issue came first on the agenda as if it were life and death and morality and prophecy. Then, if they were lucky enough to reach some completion, they moved onto the next issue with rhythmic urgency.

Dune's body sighed within, thinking ahead to being back in her bed.

Dawud had brilliantly avoided joining the council when his invite came. "In a meeting, I am the devil herself, no advocate required. I would just make everyone miserable. Plus, I'm the media, gotta stay objective."

After the meetings, he could barely stomach her downloads. If Dune said who had annoyed her, Dawud knew the rest. She still had half of her three-year term to serve; the others were just a few months ahead of her. She had so much time left in this mismatched seat of power. She tried to channel Mama Vivian, her parents, Elouise, but their fire didn't burn the same way in her.

Dune felt like a different element completely. Water flowing underground, river estranged from the sun but always searching for that warmth.

Rays of light stripped of heat filtered down into the atrium, and there was beet-berry juice being passed around the table. Dune focused on her breathing, the fastest way to shapeshift into presence . . .

Dune's Ancestor Journal, July

i always wanted to feel the deepest belonging. we always said "community is the answer to every problem." we always knew we were all connected. but we didn't realize how absolutely precious our solitude was, how much we appreciated my own individual voice and thoughts and choices. now it is a herculean task to use the word i, even to have a sense of an interior world, a self with a private inner realm. this will pass, i can feel the collective slowly becoming the main way we think. i remember sitting alone in the deliciousness of being alive and, for a moment, free in solitude. we don't want to forget it, this is what being a human is about, getting to experience the i, even though the norm is the oneness. we spent our whole singular lives trying to figure out togetherness, even though it was the essential, the familiar, the inevitable. we could have spent so much more time sitting in the quiet of the self, healing and mending the heart as an individual cell of collective life. it is hard work to be in the solitude, it is a journey to delight in the experience of being a self, to find a lasting peace in the quiet of one's own mind, in this perspective on life which is brief and the smallest part of existence. ah, even as we write this the voice i thought of as ours, as mine, is thunderous and multitude. not gone but not recognizable either.

could fall soft down
anytime, like a leaf
part of the pile
even top of the heap
i become insignificant

it is harder than dying

Fantasy

Dune lay catching her breath, letting the sun on her feet warm the rest of her body. Her hand was covered in pleasure. Her mind was sweet with the memories of her early days with Rio, when they couldn't keep their hands off each other, one act of passion continuously witnessed by friends and strangers. There was a week when all of Murmur City smelled like their bed. Now she could see faces watching her from the patterns on the ceiling tiles, but the only person she wanted to see was Rio.

Rio's pink-brown nipples, hard and alert in the half light. Rio pressing Dune's face against their chest. The sweet swamp smell of Rio's wild pussy; wet, open, clit thick as a thumb, filling up Dune's mouth. Rio rocking back and forth over Dune's tongue, between her lips. How, that first time, Dune had slipped one finger into Rio, not even a proper thrust, and Rio had shuddered in her mouth and tightened, beholden. The ritual of Rio holding Dune's head against their orgasm until they stopped shivering into her mouth.

Dune missed Rio like a limb, like flesh of her own identity. Things had gotten so strange and complicated. Rio's connection to Dune was hard on Sahari in ways other lovers hadn't been, eventually too hard to ignore. Dune now interacted with Rio as a friend, even though she knew Rio could feel the tether, however close or far they were from her. Dune admired Rio's integrity; even when they were alone together, Rio never tried to cross any boundary. They didn't kiss, didn't flirt. They hadn't even hugged in this pause.

Dune tried to stay generous with Sahari; she couldn't imagine having had Rio to herself and then having to share. Still, Sahari's stance felt like delaying something true and inevitable. How long would they have to wait? Would she ever get to taste Rio again? Get to watch them wake up and smile at her?

There was resentment, small, but steadily growing. Why be selfish now at the end of the world!?

Dune loved Rio in a different way than she loved Dawud, but a way that was equally full and important in her heart. There were no rules that would govern or stop that from being true.

Marta

Date: July 7, 2029
Subject: Testing, testing . . .

Dear Dune

I really have a strong feeling that you are alive. If you are alive just let me know—it would be nice to have something more concrete than a feeling. Unless that is how you are letting me know. But that's not like you.

I don't know if you know this yet, but H-8 might be spreading. Or I guess is being spread. The recipe for it was posted on some white hater site for like 3 minutes. Someone tried to set off a H-8 bomb on a block in Atlanta, someone else put it in the water in Oakland. The bomb apparently made people on that block sick, but they recovered. In Oakland they had to shut off the tap water. No deaths yet.

Maybe that's why I'm writing you. If you are alive, then you are like the ultimate survivor. And maybe there's something special about you that could help other people survive?

Do you know Kama is kind of famous? Patient Zero. *The ReidOut* had that Dr. Rogers on. She is on the news a lot these days. She said your mom is her biggest regret.

I don't fuck with my parents at all now. Boundaries! I am kind of alone out here, but it's better than trying to keep up with their fights and making up. I feel like each day my mind is more calm.

I miss you.
With love forever,
Marta

Hunger

Dune ate dinner alone in the dining room. A watermelon salad, greens dressed in peach vinaigrette. She made a plate to bring to Captain, and another plate for herself. She still felt hungry.

Dune looked through their snacks, longing for a pepperoni pizza, a roast beef sandwich, sushi, beef in her stew, meat. She still felt hungry.

She went to the cafe and got a snack, a little almond flour cake topped with sliced almond. She still felt hungry.

Only when Dawud pressed his weight into her did she feel full.

Landing in the Body

Mama Rue in Practice

The people needed rituals.

As it had become clear that Mama Rue's magic involved some aspect of sight and healing, and people had begun calling on her, approaching her at meals and in hallways, full of need and doubt. They called on her with open hands, side eyes, trepidation, and big, familiar questions: How do I let go? How do I make room for something good in my life? How do I remember to care for the living? How do I speak to my dead? How do we welcome a child into this new limited world? How do I trust?

She kept a bag with a variety of altar items in it: cloths of different colors and sizes, beads, stones, feathers, shells from every border where water met earth, dirt, bones, impressive leaves, bundles of cedar, pine, juniper, bowls to hold water or spells, singing bowls that rang like bells when struck or spun, tea candles, incense sticks and cones, three pendulums, and a well-worn Octavia E. Butler tarot deck. She never hurried, and she didn't seem particularly precious about her supplies. They were just on her such that when the question arose, she could tilt her head to the side and think of what was needed, fling up an altar, and bring the moment into ritual.

Mama Rue was less mystical since her semi-public transmission—her rituals were practical and often brief, she took in the need, listened for the answer, and worked in intense transmissions. Once she had felt or done or said what was needed, she quickly folded her things back into her bag with a clearing shake and left, without ceremony.

Dune had become Mama Rue's apprentice by accident. She'd been in Murmur City for six months the first time Mama Rue'd invited her over to talk about her spiritual journey. The elder wasn't a formal teacher or mentor . . . She just called Dune to come over one day and asked how she did her spells.

"I don't really know what I do. Everyone is looking at me, like I'm responsible . . . but I don't know what to do. I am nothing, I'm not my parents, I am nothing." Dune had had the feeling of accidentally confessing a secret, which she learned was part of Mama Rue's effect. This elder who called Dune to magical work was as grounded and irresistibly present as the Mama Rue Dune got in the wild was feral and foreign..

Mama Rue had responded, "You are a portal, Dune. A way somewhere is not a nothing, not at all, though it is a space. I thought you already knew that. You are a channel . . . a . . . a passage. At minimum, an important nothing. When tributaries of the river return to each other, everything flowing, they seem alien to each other. But the truth is in the returning. You are riverbanks for life, a passage through which these spirits make it home. Or other things can flow, medicine. I can show you some things to do."

In this way, Dune became the unlikely mentee to a madwoman.

....

Trailing Mama Rue for the first time on one of these spiritual rounds, Dune had been surprised to learn there was order in the old woman's chaos.

When Dune had gotten to her door, Mama Rue had handed her a canvas bag with some instruments in it and pulled the door closed behind her as she took off down the hall. They had shown up to a birth in Heart Tower. The parents were propped on the bed, support mother behind birthing mother, breathing together. There was an industrial fan blowing on them. The "doctor" was a woman named Anna who had been a nurse practitioner at Detroit Medical Center. She'd bristled a bit when Mama Rue and Dune walked in. Dune understood, trying to convey with eyes and pursed lips that they weren't there to get in anyone's way, that they had been invited, although she wasn't exactly sure that was true.

Mama Rue had rifled through the bag on Dune's shoulder until she found a Crown Royal pouch. Opening it, she'd slipped out a jade green bowl and a wooden mallet. Standing next to the parents, she'd extended her hands directly over the active belly and then held still for a moment, as if listening through her fingertips. A quick withering look at Dune was the only invitation to come around to the other side of the parents and extend her hands. Mama Rue turned Dune's palm upwards and placed the jade bowl in it. Then, Mama Rue began striking the rounded edge until the room seemed full of a deep, hollow, sweet new-life sound.

There was a quiet around the bell, as if it was hollowing out every container in the room, stilling every voice. Mama Rue eventually glanced impatiently at Dune, and as the mentee started to wonder why, she felt a song moving through her. She'd opened her mouth and begun to sing softly, "*come down baby let us hold you tight / come down baby let us catch your life / come down baby nothing else to do / oh come down baby we are ready for you.*"

As she sang this over and over, the singing bowl had gotten louder. Dune's voice was an earth pouring sound and she was surprised that she felt comfortable singing in this way—there was no sense of performance, just the function of a song that needed to be delivered.

The birthing mother began to breathe in rhythm with the song, breaths that seemed to drag knuckles along the gravel at the bottom of the world. After some time, the song moved from Dune's mouth and into the bodies in the room, which were swaying, some singing along, some rocking quietly. Even the doctor had found the rhythm of the breath. Mama Rue's eyes had closed and her face relaxed completely. A smile had come to her mouth, so brief and small that Dune almost missed it. Then the mother was shouting in long sweeps of effort and the baby was blooming from her body.

Dune had never wanted to have a child, but when she felt the threshold between life and death fill the room, she was so grateful to be able to be a part of this moment, to be a sound in it. There was a brief chaos as the baby screamed to find itself in the world, and the mothers surrounded it, love flowing through their faces and hands, laughter and weeping and gasps of awe.

After that, Dune was invited along on a Mama Rue–mission about once a week. She liked the work, the intimacy of being an extension of Mama Rue's healing instincts. It always felt immediately effective and whatever needed to happen was clear once she was there.

Mama Rue understood that Dune's voice was part of her gift,

though not the only part. Once, they stood on either side of a feverish child and breathed deeply, blowing over her with a focus on glacial cool. Another time they placed their hands under the upper body of a man who had fainted, feeling the weight of his broken heart and sharing it for a while. A trans man, struggling to find testosterone in the medicine leftover in the city's clinics, had called them to cast a gender affirmation spell over his body and spirit.

What Dune had learned, what had given her a deep sense of faith about the unseeable labor they did, was that she never ever felt a question about the usefulness of this time.

Dune's Ancestor Journal, August

we want answers
we have questions
we need to understand
you never will.

it is remarkable to even get to the question.
you live with that, or you die with that.

High

Being high and sitting in the apartment had edges. Sometimes, Dune wanted to be quiet in her high, to go inside her head. Dawud used to be able to feel when she wanted that, when she needed that. He'd understood it so inherently and immediately that Dune had never developed the capacity to ask him for it. Now he seemed to have forgotten she had a self beyond him, needs beyond his company.

She had places that were ideal to go during her high. Going out into the city alone these days was a bit spooky—in some way it felt like the spirits had claimed Detroit as the humans had claimed the Renaissance Center as Murmur City. It started to feel prickly to cross the invisible border between Murmur City and the ghost town beyond it.

She loved going to one of the gyms where she could lift weights and feel the strength in her body. She loved going to the Code Midnight Reading Room, but it only worked as a high escape room if it was mostly empty. There were so many empty rooms in the structure, so many views of the city. If she wanted to wallow, she returned to the apartment she and Rio had used as a lovers' space. Or she'd go all the way to the Tundra, far enough from others that she could truly cry and be lonely.

Sometimes, in the early morning hours, she would go to the No Trash Store. During the day other people were always in there dropping stuff off or finding treasures. The free exchange was always open because nothing cost money. For decades, during the annual Detroit Auto Show, this massive room had been a display hall for luxury cars. Now it was full of mismatched shelves and rows of stuff semi-tidily arranged on the floor, broken and unbroken, stuff people no longer wanted, things that had been worn down but could still be used by others.

Dune liked to catch and release treasures there. She was drawn to the same things over and over. Empty journals, candles, boutique soap, instruments, picture frames. She would find new items, put them in one of the mismatched rolling baskets lined up near the door. Then she would return the items, knowing she hadn't used her last hoard. The things she kept were tarot decks. She suspected that if she found the right one, Kama would be inside it.

Star Wars

Dawud was making notes for a future episode of the *Everything Awesome Circus*, which had evolved into a show with interviews of Murmur City residents. He still channeled the opening of the show, but he found the interviews helped the city feel less like a band of random survivors and more like a community. Dune was reading next to him.

"That shit is real. The dark side is real," Dawud's eyes were wide. "The hate those MFs feel towards us, that's the dark side of the force in them. We can fight them, but the harder victory is to not become them, not sink into the easy power of hatred. It's powerful, it's spiritual, it's profound! It is profound . . . I think of those stories at times like these. We got some powers—you definitely do—but not Jedi shit. Maybe 'cause we haven't figured out how to harness it yet."

"Harness it?" Dune replied, cautious. They were sitting up in bed, in the hotel suites they had claimed as a home. One suite was their bedroom and living room, the other was the main kitchen they used, and a workspace. Their bed looked out towards the river and the green wall, which seemed bright even at night.

"Yeah, like . . . don't you remember the learning-to-be-a-Jedi sequences? Montages of going from tantrum little bitchboy to grounded unflappable warrior with a lightsaber?"

"Boy or girl." Dune responded factually and Dawud accepted the correction with a quick nod.

"You think we should be training to fight?"

"Well . . . kind of? They trained, but actually the fight part was decentered—they had to learn to tap into the force and wield it, stay focused, like, kind of partner with it."

Dune felt annoyed when Dawud did this kind of didactic aside, where she had to really listen between his words to find out what he was trying to tell her. Out the window, big, gorgeous summer storm clouds were dumping a lake's worth of water straight down, quelling Dune's impulse to escape. Slightly trapped, she engaged.

"But my shift happens when I'm asleep. And it might not even be a power. It might just be my mom."

Dawud was quiet for long enough that Dune started reading again.

"Have you heard of lucid dreaming?" He was pulling at a thread in the middle of the blanket.

"Yes. Top-five activity for white people." Dune pulled his hand away from the thread.

Dawud scoffed, catching her wrist. "Does it hurt when you try to fit your genius into such a narrow world view?"

"I have literally *never* heard of a Black person doing that." Dune was covering her own tracks. She had *A Field Guide to Lucid Dreaming* and *Of Water and the Spirit: Ritual, Magic, and Initiation in the Life of an African Shaman* under her side of the bed, desperately trying to learn to dream her way to Kama. She spun her wrist upwards.

"Well, my mom did that. Super Black." Dawud pulled Dune's wrist up to his lips and kissed it. "Black people have always done everything humans have done. Our people have dream traveled that way for ages. What you know about African dream root? That shit predates any European experiments in lucid dreaming."

"You better get your the-more-you-know-head-ass out of here with that shit." Dune snapped back with a smirk, but she didn't pull away from his lips, and she made a mental note to research this dream root.

Dawud was laughing, unbothered. He held her palm against his face, looking playful. "So, ok, you the one moving houses in your sleep. You the one building walls made of vines around the whole ass city. You, the untamed Jedi. But I'm the one who needs to chill? Aight."

Dune pulled her hand back, getting grumpy, clearly bothered. "Well shit, I must have missed the movie where the Jedi lucid dream their way to victory."

Dawud looked at Dune as if just seeing her, taking in her frustration, her crossed arms, her doubt. He reached over and pulled her hair, too friendly, and she started fake pummeling his belly.

He grabbed her hands and held her against him, wanting her to take charge of him. She understood the mission and flipped him away from her, pushing him down onto the bed. She stepped into her strap, used her spit as lubrication, and fucked her frustration out. Afterwards, he slid two fingers into her and sucked her left nipple, the more sensitive one, which she sometimes called her dick, as in "suck my . . ." Where the sensations met, she came undone, and for a brief moment, in the clarity of orgasm, she felt that he was right. She needed to harness her power if she was going to keep them safe.

At minimum she would watch the *Star Wars* movies again.

Dune's Ancestor Journal, August

we live through the unimaginable, that's what it means to be human. what matters is finding your own peace inside of that. which is impossible because the unimaginable is humanity, it is the result of our existence. so most people, at some point, they become aware that there's one true binary in this world. you are either mending or breaking the future.

most of us are doing both at the same time because we aren't designed to hold one half of a contradiction. we hold both halves, and we hold them with shame. the good is never good enough, or good for long enough. the bad is the worst, but you can also explain it, which makes you lose faith in the whole shitshow.

i had my heart broken really early. someone i trusted touched me and it made me sick. sick in the moment, each moment. but also sick in the head, cause you gotta contort your brain to keep going. you're young so you handle trauma like cleaning your room, push everything under the bed and into the closet and smile. the door closes? must be manageable.

i had too much stuff, so i tried to get bigger than the sharp edges, i jerry-rigged a bungee cord, i duct-taped the perimeter, i expanded like belly flesh around a pressing fetus foot. shit i even felt miraculous because i could tell it was a good life. didn't even have to enjoy it to know that.

and then i met someone who didn't flinch when i did, who pulled me closer when i cried, who found the seduction in the small space between birth and heaven. i had nothing to offer but pieces and he approached me as a multitude. to me, this too was unimaginable.

Dune in Her Body

Dune walked into the kitchen, thirsty from sexual labor. Topping Dawud was a more intense outpouring of energy than she had ever given before. She generally enjoyed the workout, the sweat dripping down her back, slicking the space between them. But tonight she felt out of shape, not quite herself in the motion. Her naked reflection caught her, staring from the closed refrigerator, elongated.

She had been avoiding herself in the mirror as she gained weight, not exactly in aversion, but with an inability to face one more change. She knew she was eating more, often more than her body could even hold, but the weight gain still felt surprising, like her body betraying a private moment. In the bathroom, she brushed her teeth looking down, sliding her feet over the cool tiles. Moving through Murmur City, where everything was made of glass and reflections, she had gotten good at softening her eyes, seeing something more general and diluted than her own form. Inside her skin, she felt the same as ever, like the virus had changed everything in the world but her.

Now, Dune looked at the soft curve of her chin, disoriented. The strap hung down from under her spilling pale belly, her thighs touching behind the brown silicone, her breasts heavier, areolas lighter and wider.

Her budding masculinity had been hard, slender, strong. Could she be her boi self, her true self, in this soft body? Could she love this soft body? This question happened in her, too deep to be seen directly. She reached across the kitchen counter for a half-smoked joint and finished it, her back to the refrigerator. She slipped *Star Wars: Return of the Jedi* into Dawud's DVD player. She didn't return to bed—she needed time not in reach of anyone, in any way.

Love Stories

Dune's Ancestor Journal, August

head over heels. that's how i left this world, in a state of erotic and emotional bliss. i wasn't sad much. no, that's a lie. i was sad, i was angry, i was terrified. but that was brief, only once i realized i was dying. before that, i was so happy.

i grew up convinced i was not worthy of love. can you believe it? i mean i am not the fool who says everyone is worthy: i have met some people who came into this world and chose violence. i don't pretend to know why the universe keeps perpetuating that way of being, but here we are. i was a sweet kid, a good daughter, a smart student, and i always tried to do right by people. i just wasn't pretty in the ways humans decided was pretty. i was very pretty if you weren't all messed up by those small decisions often made by people's own narrow desire, not what they could attain, not what they even looked like themselves.

i don't deny that there are certain looks and forms that seem to dazzle, to delight the eye. i had a large head, a big spacious face, small pert lips, small breasts, a large soft belly, a flat tucked ass, and legs that looked chiseled from stone. none of my curves were in the places that men were trained to seek them, so even though there was so much softness and so much that was hard, i grew up thinking it was an impossible body to love.

and when i met her, when i met the woman who met my eyes and already loved me, it was a revelation. she wasn't pretty either, she was fine. we were fine and we looked at each other like scholars. i didn't know what it felt like to be seen—you don't even really know what it is like to be alive until someone sees you and looks at you as both an object they want and a soul they need. it matters, to be wanted that way. it mattered to me.

i think there is more freedom for those of us who don't fit neatly into the box of pretty. we get to try more things. we know earlier that the impression we make on the world is one we can shape. i let my weird go wild under her gaze, and she came into her own great power.

we didn't get enough time and i'm not sure we ever would have, if we had lived from the beginning of existence to the end.

dying as i did, so suddenly, i feel incomplete. a half-formed thought. a sentence on the tip of a tongue. i don't know if she misses me or if she is also here in the everything. i feel her, but i can't tell anything about the feeling—present or past, close or far, living or dead. it feels constant, but i don't. i am learning how to become distinct enough in myself to do ancestor work. maybe then i can find her and tell her goodbye, or become one spirit with her. i want to thank her, even though i said it a million times and showed her gratitude and worship in every choice i made. the humility of being loved the way she loved me reverberates beyond lifetimes. it is a song i never want to stop singing.

Dune found the wistful smile on her lips as she finished channeling, and then she went to where Dawud was watching the Studio Ghibli DVD *Spirited Away*. She curled up next to him, mindful of a desire to climb not just into his arms, but fold directly into his skin.

Berta

In the two years that Dune had lived in Murmur City, Berta was one of the miracles who had appeared.

Bineshii, a leader from the Anishinaabe peoples who lived on Wawiiatanong Isle, had brought Berta to a Murmur City healing exchange. People with healing methods to offer gathered in the ballroom and Dune moved in a crowd of people around the circuit. There had been about thirty tables in the room, humaned by healers who offered acupuncture, massage therapy, meditation, yoga, reiki, tarot cards, tinctures and herbal medicine, talk therapy, mediation, facials, nail care, and other things.

Berta had been sitting with a table of women from Wawiiatanong Isle who had offerings on the table—art, medicine bundles, testimonials. Berta's face had brightened in some subterranean recognition when Dune approached, and she reached out to take Dune's hand. As soon as they touched, Dune could feel that Berta was a powerful healer, a river of calm pouring from Berta into Dune's hand and flowing through her entire body and down through the soles of her feet.

They had met once a week since then, on the third floor of Owl Song where no one would hear their labor. Berta was training Dune to move energy through her body. Sometimes she held space for Dune to have full-body shaking releases—releases of grief, of the traumas of losing her mother and her city to H-8, the trauma of losing her father to a bus accident, and other losses wound tight in her cellular structure. Sometimes Dune held space for Berta's releases, which took a different shape, with Dune's hands just holding the back of Berta's head while the healer trembled and wept under a blanket. Sometimes the two women just talked, formally deciding who would be the focal point, or if there was time and capacity for mutual support.

About six months into the work, debriefing a massive opening for Dune, they realized they had come across a black hole of terror that might have been passed down to Dune from Kama's body, in birth or in death. This was a theory, because the details were elusive, which was common for embodied trauma. Whenever Berta spent time around Dune's solar plexus, Dune saw shadowy figures coming through a doorway, and started hyperventilating.

While living in California, Berta had trained in somatic bodywork. She was one of the tiny number of Detroiters who had returned to the city after H-8 had started, before the wall. After avoiding the initial waves of evacuation, her family had taken over a set of empty homes in Lafayette Park because it was so green there. Her parents were part of the Free the Land crew. They had created a prioritized plan for decolonizing Detroit, which mostly involved stewarding the land back to wilderness by removing toxic chemicals and materials from homes and buildings that were on track to be reclaimed by nature.

It had taken a year of meetings between the Mbongi Council and the Wawiiatanong delegates to co-create the Free the Land project, which included thinking together through the healthiest use of existing agricultural and green spaces. Dune and Berta were silent about the business between their peoples, which allowed them to traverse territory that was both more intimate and shared: their broken hearts and their outsized healing powers.

....

Now Dune lay on the floor, with Berta sitting close to her left shoulder like an angel. Dune could feel where Berta was sitting, feeling the unique heat and pulse of light in her body. Hearing the rhythm of her breath dancing with the heartbeat. Opening her energy, Dune invited Berta past the barriers between them, to come with her and look at the past. Dune could see flashes of detail from her own history, without knowing the emotional texture, intensity, or any kind of chronological order. Pain was nonlinear, the pattern a chaos of wounds. Berta saw knots in a pattern of energy, places that were swollen and red, or purple, or greenish gray. She could bring her own energy to flow to one of these points of inflammatory memory and Dune could feel the attention and just soften there, breathe just there, allowing whatever was held to move. Sometimes she saw or felt distinct images, moments, actions. Lately it was an emotional imprint, a feeling of terror and needing to get smaller that didn't come with any clear story or image.

Today Berta thought they could learn more about that visceral fear. Berta found the emotion and flowed into it, feeling the grand tenderness of such an ancient bruise in spirit. The wound felt eternal. Berta's flesh hands gripped ever so slightly and then they both felt that Berta held the wound in her hands. On the table Dune felt nauseous, cold and sweaty. Then she was gripped by the emotional reality of the wound. Someone was looking for her; when they found her they were going to rip her body apart.

She felt so little compared to the one who was looking for her. But not little enough.

Dune began to whimper and curl up smaller and smaller on her side, trying to protect her face and her belly and heart all at once. Berta threw a blanket over Dune and added her own body weight as a protector. Dune began to quiver, and Berta knew the knot was coming apart.

"What is your name?" Berta whispered, leaning over Dune and watching her face. Dune's eyelids squeezed tight and then flew open, showing wild, not-at-all-Dune's eyes. Berta smiled at the lost one, who seemed impossibly young, who had clearly been caught in a painful contortion for longer than Dune's lifetime. Berta opened the floodgates of her palms, flowing her force into Dune, partnering with Dune to move this weighted spirit out of her. After a period of time that felt like both seconds and hours, there was a fluttering of energetic wings, followed by a feeling of chaos leaving the room. To the spirit, to herself, and to Dune, Berta said, "You are free. Your work here is done."

Turn Off

It was Dune's night to serve dinner while Dawud and Jizo dined with Captain. The dinner crew each night was forty people split between food prep, cooking, serving, and clean-up. Everyone able to serve in Murmur City was responsible for about twenty nights of kitchen crew a year, and depending who else was on shift, it could be a really fun assignment.

Tonight, Dune was moving large, hot, covered trays from the kitchen into the dining room, slotting them down into silver serving tables heated by water. As she got her second tray settled, she looked up to find Rio next to her, on the same task. Dune felt the familiar rush of sensations and curiosities flush through her system. She took a deep self-regulating breath. Rio smiled, as if to herself, but Dune heard it like a sentence.

After the shift, Rio offered to walk Dune home. They walked close and talked small, not touching in any way that mattered. As they reached the elevators of Dune's building, Dune stopped.

"Rio what are we doing?" Dune's hand pointed to the space between their bodies. She was truly confused.

"I'm holding a boundary to protect someone who doesn't deserve to be hurt." Rio tried to say this gently, but it wasn't gentle inside them; they felt caught in someone else's boundaries.

"And what about me?" Dune's face showed that she was trying to keep this conversation light, though it wasn't. "Do I deserve to be hurt? Do I deserve to have less of you? Do I deserve to be horny all the time? What about me?"

People were approaching them, so Rio started walking around the elevator bank, onto the path that circled the whole floor in a strange floating glass track. Dune kept up, needing answers.

"What about you?" Rio sounded incredulous. "What about me? I'm the one making this sacrifice. I'm the one who has to spend my life unsatisfied. I'm the one who has to watch you move around the city, untouchable to me. I'm the one generating love in a space where I no longer feel it in that way." Rio looked pained, uncomfortable, righteous.

Dune let some disgust show. "That's what you're *choosing* to do. But why? Can you explain it to me again? I know you think this is the right move. And I really want to honor your integrity and honor your kindness and honor your heart. But the thing Sahari is so scared of has already happened. It happened when we met. If we are in the same room, we are together; there is something wild between us."

Rio paused and smiled briefly, caught off guard. They sobered up, started walking again. "Baby, understand me—I stay. I've never been the one to leave. That's why I'm here now, in this city that died all around me. I didn't leave, I didn't make the selfish move. I'm here and I'm with Sahari."

Dune received this like a left hook; she was amazed she could keep walking. For a while they held the silence.

"Ok. I accept that. I accept that this is your choice, but it means I have to fully let you go. You said you were open when we met, that's why I let it get this far. Then you said wait, so I have been waiting. I'm not waiting anymore. Maybe you have some beautiful idea in your head that some time in the future you'll find a way to make this transition not hurt. But I guarantee you she already hurts. There is no right time, there's just wasted time. There are just days that turn into weeks that turn into years of not being happy and us not being together. And we are going to live those days either way, but I . . . I can't keep waiting for you."

"I didn't know you *were* waiting for me. You never told me that."

"Rio, you said you need to handle Sahari in the right way. That *this* love was home. What did you mean by that?"

"I mean that I made a commitment to her, to ride out the apocalypse together. Sahari has a lot of trauma, it's her business. So even though you feel like home to me, I have to handle her with care. What do you want from me?"

"Clarity. All I've wanted this whole time was clarity. You never told me you chose her."

"Baby, I didn't choose her. I love you both, it just hurts her too much for you and I to have a sexual relationship. I'm giving you everything else I can."

"You have given me nothing for so long that I can't remember the last time we were alone together. But . . . even if this 'everything' you speak of *was* being given, are you saying she's Ok with that? Knowing that you want me and that you're denying yourself what you want in order to uphold your commitment to her? That's love?"

Rio looked distraught, the closest Dune had ever seen them to tears. "Isn't it love? Isn't love about staying? Unconditionally? No matter what comes, no matter the conditions, no matter the temptations—isn't that love?"

"Not the kind that you and I could have." Dune felt heartbreak open up underneath her, dropping from fantasy into reality. "You and I tasted freedom, Rio. We know that love can be freedom. I know you know that."

"Dune, that freedom is still possible. You want me to settle for sharing your love with someone else, but you won't share mine with someone else? You're not leaving Dawud, you never even offered. You say you love him and love me. He doesn't care about sex like that, so you don't have to limit anything. You're lucky; you hit the apocalypse jackpot. I have a different situation. I don't see why this has to keep us from each other, I don't understand."

"Dawud doesn't mind the sexual part because he knows he doesn't own my body and that, for any of my relationships to be real, I have to be allowed to be me. That's why his relationship with me is so generous, so spacious. It's not easy, but it's worth it. He trusts my love." Mostly.

"Well, Sahari isn't wired that way. And I don't know that that will ever change for her. And I do . . . care about her." Dune and Rio could both hear the uncertainty in Rio's voice.

"Ok. Ok."

"Ok what? What if you trusted *my* love? What if you trusted that we didn't have to be having sex to love each other?"

"That sounds crazy. Something about this just feels slippery."

"Damn. Couples go through shit where they can't have sex. And, somehow, they stay together for fifty years."

"We're not going through shit. We're both perfectly healthy, we're both adults, and we desire each other. Like the nature of our relationship is a sexual relationship, a romantic relationship, a relationship where we are kissing and holding each other and part of our communication, a divine part, is the part that happens between our bodies. Even right now, I know you can feel me."

"But that's my point exactly. You know I can feel you, why does it matter *how* I feel you?"

"Because! It's . . . it's a turn off, Rio! It's a turn off to think that you can feel this desire the way I do, and then let someone else dictate the terms of our engagement. Why don't you fight for us? Why don't you fight for *our* right to exist? Like . . . you must not feel what I feel!"

"Ok, you want the truth? I'm scared I'll lose her." Rio's fear shone on their face. "It's lonely surviving everyone you love. It's lonely. What you're offering me is a portion of your love. She's offering me all of hers. She doesn't say I can't talk to you, can't be friends with you. It just can't be a romantic relationship."

Dune looked at Rio, as if a look between them could change everything that was being said. Then Dune looked away. Rio grabbed Dune's shoulders, risking the brief touch to let their feelings pour directly into their beloved.

"Don't give up on us. I know it's not the way you want it to be, but I love you. And I'm alive. And we don't know what happens next."

Captain and Pork

"Dawud, why you always on that show talking about pork fat bacon?" Captain asked from the conference table that had been repurposed as a dining room table for Captain and Jizo's apartment. Every surface was thick with precious items from Captain's life: propped up framed photos of him and Delilah, trophies and medals and photo albums and news clippings and art. The clash between Captain's Black cultural artifacts and the neutrality of the office always amused Dune. "Did y'all know there was a time when I didn't eat pork?"

Jizo made a concerned face.

"*How to Eat to Live*, huh? I read that too," Dawud chuckled from the kitchen where he and Dune were cooking breakfast. The kitchen counters were covered in summer spoils—piles of lettuce, a sparse bowl of eggs, a basket of strawberries, a thawing package of plant protein, a hill of small green onions.

Captain looked surprised and pleased, listening with his mouth just a little bit open, his next story primed. Dawud continued, "I think if I hadn't grown up on the sweet perfection of bacon, I would have gone Muslim in my twenties." He caught Dune's look of doubt and shrugged into it, "Impressionable kid, rigor fetish." He saw Captain, full of answers to an unasked question. "What brought you back?"

"Oh I was influenced by the Nation, that was f'certain. For a while, to be *Black*, to be *Conscious*, you needed to hold on to some shared shit, some discipline. That one felt good. But then the day I got laid off . . . it was the end of the world for me. My world. I had my Delilah, my love, and my job. My coworkers were my people, we shared everything with each other, complained together, drank together—we believed in each other. Then Ford laid me off. Like I was nothing, like the years I gave them was nothing." Captain's eyes grew soft as he looked through time.

"When I left the military, it was with honor. Cause I had served my time. I know I wasn't the smartest or the fastest. But I showed all the way up. Every day. I approached making 'em cars the same way. Serving my country, serving this need we had, this growth we was engaged in. Together. It was a thing that gave me so much pride. To be part of the 'American work force,' to buy *our* house." He paused here and laughed, as they all thought of the house that had moved itself to blend their family.

"That whole thing was ours. Outright. And we had our own car," his chin moved up and his smile weighed down on the edges with pride. "That was why Sundays were created, to drive a gorgeous woman around in the sunshine after saying hello to God. They didn't even say nothing, they didn't even tell me I was no longer needed, thank you for the years in service to they dream. They gave me a pink slip of paper, me and a thousand others. The day started one way, ended another. My world ended that day. And I was driving home, kind of driving all over the city in a daze, heartbroken really, heart just broken. What was I gonna tell Delilah? How was I gonna look in her face? So I stop by the meat joint at Eastern and got some ribs. Now Delilah, that woman could cook some ribs up just right, and I had denied it to her on my righteous tip. So I bring home a rack of ribs and I say, 'Baby girl, things done changed for us today.' My concept of *myself* had changed. And she cooked up those ribs and I thought about who I needed to be. And that was a philosopher, a historian of this city, of the movements that shaped this city. Man, it's all in here." Captain tapped his temple, smiling and full of treasure.

Dune placed bowls in the middle of the table—faux bacon, sliced strawberries, and herbed eggs. They all started eating, knowing how to make the small portions cover each plate.

Thresholds

Everything Awesome Circus
"The sweet sweet sound of my beloved is echoing through the empty halls of Murmur City because we outsiiiiiiiide boy! Hello beloved cockatoos and aardvarks, mosquitoes and wasp nests, wind tunnels and rainstorms, locusts and loud-as-fuck cicadas. Like, why is summer the loudest season? Is everyone calling out 'I Am Hot As Fuck!' at the same time? We living in rewilding time and I feel the fur all over my spirit. I hear it calling out to me, a future that lives just under the present, ever rising, ever splitting open the dying world with a green root and an unruly possibility. The future I hear has the rhythms of a past I recall in my cells, but I never saw it, never smelled it, and so every day I watch us make a memory that is only right because we all feel the rightness. Let the crowd say axé and woah-meeeen.

"My guest today is Leonard Makwa, from the Waawiiatanong delegation. Leonard, what indeed is good?"

"Boozhoo niijiikiiwenh. Niminwendaan gaganoozhinaan noongom. Bkejwanong indoonjibaa. Omaa gichi-odenaang aw ingii-tazhi nitaawigi'igoo. Detroit izhinkaazod zhaaganaashiimong. Waabziiminis indaa noongom, 'Belle Isle' izhinikaazod. What I shared there in my language is that I'm happy to be speaking with you today. I come from Walpole Island, or what we call Bkejwanong, 'the place where the water divides.' Bkejwanong describes the freshwater delta that sits at the center of our nation's territory. I grew up here in this big city known as Detroit. And I live on Swan Island, or 'Belle Isle' as it's called. Thank you for the honor of having me here in your Circus. Today is a very good day, a special day to be with you."

"Man, I am glad you came, and that you are willing to keep talking to my ignant ass. Ok, so my first question for you is, what do you wish the people of Murmur City understood better about our Anishinaabe hosts?"

"I like how you asked that, Brother Dawud. Because even just the acknowledgement that we are hosts, that we have a relationship with the land that precedes the current crisis, is something I wish was understood more widely. That we have had many moments here when it felt like an ending, a beginning. And initially, in this crisis of hate, we were torn between rooting and migrating. We landed on staying, really turning inwards to understand what the dreams are for this place, the dreams of the land, the dreams of all our relations here."

"Yeah, I noticed that, when we came to Murmur City y'all wasn't here. Like not sleeping here, even though you were involved."

"You know a lot of people didn't even pick up on that. Because to notice we were gone they'd have to have noticed we were still here. So, I appreciate you picking up on that, even if it's just because you are surveillance-brained from your time in the white man's ARMY." The men's laughter tangled together, mangrove roots. "Now, on your original question though, the other thing I want people to understand, because people love to romanticize us, is that we weren't perfect. And anyone who tried to claim that is hustling you. But we had and have a different orientation to place, to time, to our days, to our dead. Our orientation is guided by relationship, first with the Earth. There is no time in the past, present, or future in which everyone just sat around in teepees. We had nomads, hunters, weavers, artisans, we traded, we mapped and studied our territories. We had adventures and romance and quarrels and differences and addiction and sadness and multi-tribal relationships."

"Right, you're saying there isn't some static universal 'Indian' way."

"Yeah, there are many belief systems amongst the First, Aboriginal, Indigenous peoples of the world. What makes us unique is not that we have these belief systems. It is that we have been able to sustain them through genocide, displacement, miseducation, and erasure. When I share a principle with you from my people, or sing you one of our songs, it is a treasure because it is something I can offer you, intact, after all of those struggles. You, I call you my brother. And what I mean by this is that we are both in the same family of persecution. When I hear you enter your state of wisdom, I know it is a channel directly from the Creator, a channel that has survived in you, despite every effort to destroy it."

"You getting me choked up, man."

"That's also a victory. Warriors are most successful when we can harness our emotions—our anger fuels our resistance, our broken heartedness and missing our mothers and wanting to impress our fathers and all of it, we harness that into our power. Think of water—water can be powerful in so many forms, because it denies itself no form. We are water, so when we say a blessing for the waters moving through the world we are also meant to bless the water moving through us, which is sometimes a river and sometimes ice and sometimes hail and sometimes vapor. But always us, always life moving towards life."

"That's deep. I have been feeling like swamp water, some kind of murky water, but this is making me think about that differently, like this is a natural state."

"Absolutely! How would you not be murky, muddy, thick with sediment and run off and churning waste? Part of colonizer legacy is that we have forgotten how to think. How to ask questions. How to see ourselves and others with compassion. How to care for ourselves as a part of the land. You have to think something is valuable to treat it with care. So the water is great as an example, a metaphor, a case study, and a self-examination. The water was being mistreated for so long. Now it seems to have been the way your people were attacked. But water has also been a savior before—for your people the swamp once looked like heaven, from the perspective of slavery it was the only freedom. Around the world people ask the water to carry them and their children to freedom, to something better. We pray the rain will douse the parched earth and put out the fire that has lost its way. Right now is a water time, the world will be cleansed, it is a time to sing thank you to the water you drink and bathe in, a time for water ceremony, a time to care for the water and protect the water. Which includes you, the dirty water."

"Water time huh. That feels really clear, really accessible. Thank you, Leonard. Ok I have a different question for you. A lot of people died here. I mean since there were people here, we have struggled to live, especially to live in any kind of peace. But we are approaching three years since the fastest and most fatal crisis . . ."

"I have to interrupt you there, Dawud."

"Get me together."

"I want to caution us against ever saying something is the *most*, the *worst*, the *biggest*, these kinds of words. If you see that the whole world is relational, then you must know that the suffering of loss is also relative. You have grief, or you don't have grief—to say who has the most is to try and measure something immeasurable."

"Ah, so like in the past it might have been less people, but just as fatal?"

"Yes. A genocide feels like genocide, regardless of the scale of the community. The depth of the wound is intended to eradicate existence. I am not saying this to diminish what has happened here, the brutality of our Black relatives being targeted and murdered, the totality of the plan. But if you put those words in there, 'the most,' 'the worst,' then something in me catches on defensiveness, and instead of feeling our solidarity, I feel some unhealthy competition of suffering."

"Wow, Leonard, I get this. I get this. Because basically what happened here is that Black people experienced what the Anishinaabe experienced before us."

"Exactly. Now we sit together as creatures who have survived being hunted by the same predator. And the predator is not the body, the white body, the white man. The predator is the idea that we can somehow live our lives without being in relationship to the Earth. And this predator hunts us from within, you know. It allows for this violent dehumanization. To get to the place where someone takes the time and uses their intelligence to create a method for killing others—not for food, not for honor, just for some sense of domination—that is always a tragedy. But then to specify. That a people, because of where they were born, because of what their skin makes you feel, that those people don't deserve access to life, to just try at life like anyone else. Because it's not like being alive is easy or in any way a guaranteed good thing. But it is a chance at a good thing, it is a chance for moments of beauty and connection and miracle. When you take that away from people based on their race, or their ethnicity, that means you have completely disconnected yourself from the good river of life."

"You're saying the tragedy is within the one doing the harm?"

"Yes. And again, not to diminish the impact. It hurts, it is devastating and dangerous to be preyed upon by your own species. But to become a predator, to be used by a predatory idea, the spiritual weight of that is unbearable. We think the whole societal crisis is the result of falling out of a relational way of seeing the world. Everything is out of balance." Leonard's hands had been up and wide for some time, but Dawud only noticed now how it felt like all of existence was in Leonard's hands.

"You are blowing my mind right now, man," Dawud was smiling, but his eyes flooded. "Preyed upon, I can feel that in my gut, I feel that when I think about what happened to my sister and to thousands of Black people here. We were preyed upon. And before we lost contact with the outside, it sounded like a wave of white suicides were increasing the number of people impacted by this thing. So that's what I was trying to ask—is it possible to have too many people die at once . . . and how do we relate to all those . . . ghosts?"

"Death is a part of the life cycle. It is meant to be a form of freedom in a cycle of learning. Being bound into a particular life and then freed back to the earth to grow with it. Imagine that the body is a seed, death is a blooming. The body gives back to the earth, the spirit blossoms and travels back to the spirit realm. So, one thing is to recognize when that many people die that quickly, a lot of spirits might be caught. So we have to help those ancestors sometimes, to find their home to the spirit world."

Dawud's fingertips sorted the air as he responded, "I heard once that, like, Voodoo homies think of trees as these portals between the spirit world and the material one. Maybe anything wild can be a portal. Like when you see something that reminds you of an ancestor, consider that *that is* your ancestor in that moment. That ancestors just need dirt and an invitation to grow."

"Well, that is one way to understand it. Another way is to see that everything is carrying the great spirit, which longs to be whole. Coming into the human experience is unique because we can *think* we are outside the whole. But ancestors know their entire lineage in every direction, and they remember the original instructions of care, love, relationship. When two lineages meet in one body, they just hold instructions for more places, they can maybe see the patterns differently. Most of the two-leggeds now carry instructions for many places. Ancestors in the spirit world are trying to help us. We can release them and honor them by listening to the wisdom of the dirt. How present can you be with what is?"

"How present can we be with what is? Ok, Circus? You hear that? That is the assignment. 'Be here now' and listen. Plant the ancestors in your world like trees—"

"Not *like* trees Dawud. *Plant* trees. Plant actual trees. Plant everything you can plant and help it grow. And share it. We are going to share with Murmur City soon a protocol for this land. But I can tell you already that it is mostly to add to the wilderness and get everything out of the way that is not life moving towards life. So probably you gotta get out of this building."

"Bet! And plant trees. You making me feel like a tree."

"That's the best way to feel, brother. As we close, can I read you a poem? It is from one of my favorite ancestors, John Trudell. I'll just read a portion of it that helps me when I forget.

> *Listen to us impatient one*
> *We are forever*
> *You must remember the gentleness of time*
> *You are struggling to be who you are*
> *You say you want to learn the old ways*
> *Struggling to learn*
> *When all you must do is remember*
> *Remember the people*
> *Remember the sky and earth*
> *Remember the people*
> *Have always struggled to live*
> *In harmony in peace*

"'All you must do is remember.' Bars. Let the people say axé—actually what do y'all say at the end of a conversation?"

"Baamaapii, gigaawaabaamin miinwaa," Leonard said with a grin.

"That shit right there," Dawud was smiling too. "Thank you for being with us, brother."

Pouch

Mama Rue's space seemed to be a portal to a slightly different planet. It smelled like dirt, mystery, iron, and citrus. It was simultaneously clean and filled to the brim; diaphanous veils swooped down from the ceiling and softened the light. Dune stood in the foyer, looking out the window ahead, which was just the wall of green. It felt for a moment that there was a jungle inside and out.

"What you want?" Mama Rue was wiping a kitchen countertop, hard, as if it had harmed her with its mess.

"Dream root."

Mama Rue briefly showed surprise. Dune always felt some sense of victory when she could get a real-time emotional reaction from the witch. Mama Rue set down the sponge, washed her hands, and disappeared into the shadows of the apartment. Dune stayed still; her feet knew she didn't have permission to really enter. As she stood there, she noticed two things. One was that there were several piles of books that seemed unstable, the ones on the top too big for those on the bottom but somehow still standing. Two, the wall of vines outside Mama Rue's window had a few patches of yellow and orange on it. The first year of following the wall through seasons had been shocking. Now, Dune was just caught off guard by the pace of time. Wasn't it just winter? And now, again, fall.

When Mama Rue returned, she was holding a small pouch and looked frustrated. "I don't see the dream root, but this blend will give you more power to make decisions in your dreams—close enough. There's three nights of journey in here." She frowned at the pouch in her hand, then looked up at Dune with something akin to intrigue. "Don't do them back-to-back. Take it with tea at dinner and just go ahead to sleep."

Dune accepted the pouch, a ton of questions quiet in her mouth. She could feel that Mama Rue was already moving along with her day. She slipped back out into the hallway, which suddenly felt frosty and far from everyone she knew.

Root

That night, Dune made the tea with a spoonful out of the pouch, not mentioning it to Dawud, partially because she didn't want him to feel any kind of victory. When she felt a wave of nausea, she smoked a joint to calm her belly, only thinking halfway through it that maybe being high with the dreamroot-esque potion was questionable.

She started doing the dishes, already feeling heavy with the coming sleep, when Dawud stepped behind her, pressing his whole body against her, breathing into her neck. She half turned, enough to kiss him.

"Don't stop the dishes," he whispered, unbuckling his belt. He pulled down her sweatpants, rubbing against her, his fingers outside her boxer briefs, until she was ready. Every time she paused in her washing to receive his stroke, he would remind her to stay on task, his tone gruff. She rarely got this Dawud, insistent to top her—he was strange to her, compelling. She kept trying to wash the dishes until she broke a plate. Dawud cut a finger pushing it out of the way, and she put it in her mouth, licking the droplet of blood slowly. The look of surprised arousal on his face was new. He whispered, "Nasty," in her ear as he slammed into her. They came together.

When she finally reached the bed, she fell asleep immediately, her tongue tasting of iron. Her dreams started quickly. A Black boy child was running towards her. She immediately recognized him as Dawud. He was crying about something unimportant, and she scooped him up and put him on her hip, understanding that she was his grandmother. She made him laugh and it was a laugh she knew. She realized she wanted to see him at every age. She set him down and kneeled in front of him. She touched his face and he smiled at her, a big cheesy uninhibited grin. He grew in front of her eyes, to be a teenager, to be a young man. Somewhere in those years he stopped smiling as he grew into the man she knew now. She wanted to ask him what happened, but he kept growing, kept aging, so handsome. She saw the gray fill into his disappearing hair, the lines fold into his face.

She felt love for every iteration of him.

Dune's Ancestor Journal, September

i'm not a writer, i'm not a memoirist; we have never before felt like we had a story to tell. but now i'm in this other world where i can feel what used to be layered on top of what is. and we can feel what's coming, layered just below. and it feels like it's worthy of documentation. we tell it all straight, then lose the pages over and over—but we still have to tell it.

we are kama. i am, and i'm a mother, a wife, a daughter-in-law, and i was once a daughter. i was once alone, but now i can't say for sure. i have known a lot of love in my life, but now i can't touch any of those loved ones. can we still love them even if they can't see us? if they can't hear me? i feel like i'm behind a thick fog inside myself. i've always been the one to keep going, to keep moving despite all the signs and symbols telling me to be still. now, all the signs are saying to move, to act, to go, to do, to intervene, to shape, to change, to manifest. but i can't seem to move at all, i miss my daughter, i miss my breath. where am i? what am i? today my husband visited me. i know that he's dead, but i'm not convinced that i am. that made the visit even more intriguing. i wasn't surprised to see him and that surprised me. he showed up while i was sitting down by the pond—there's a pond in my backyard here, which i'm not sure was there before, but those are the kind of questions i deal with now. my dead husband came and sat by the pond with me today to have a talk. he said there's some thing that i need to do. there's something that only i can do. i felt angry with him, which i try to never feel because i miss him so much. but seeing him again and him telling me there was something i needed to do, it made me so angry. it made me wanna fight him. it made me wanna yell at him. i never yelled at him in life, although i did get frustrated and wish he would change. but now i've lived all these years without him and now he wants to tell me something else i have to do? doesn't he know how impossible these years have been? can he even comprehend how angry and sad and confused and shaken each day has been in his absence?

he was supposed to be here.

he was supposed to share all this labor of family with me. he was supposed to help me figure out what to do about his mom. he was supposed to know how to balance out the energies our child needed. he was supposed to help us be stable. instead, i, the aries, i've had to somehow make a way out of no way for us. and i don't know that i did a good job.

maybe that's why we're still sitting here.

maybe we're here in this halfway house of the soul because we weren't good enough at loving, or good enough at organizing, or good enough at gathering people to move towards a compelling future.

maybe i didn't grieve well enough all that i lost.

maybe it's because we were a rebellious daughter?
maybe we wanted too much.
maybe i took too much joy, too much pleasure.
what could we have done differently?
how could we have given more of myself?
did we miss some sign?
did we miss the moment where my purpose became clear?
did we miss the moment where our love was required?
is that why i'm here?

no, i've gone wandering again. this keeps happening. it's so hard to keep a thread, a thought, in this place. i sat down to write this because my husband came to visit me today and he shook me to my core.

he's here, my child is not.
he's dead, but my child is not.
so where are we?

he says i have work to do ... but so far, he won't tell me what the work is. this infuriates me! i want messages from spirit to be direct; i have to grieve so much just to hear them.

Hoka

"Something on your mind?"

Hoka somehow looked younger each day. Being here amongst so many people with so much purpose was giving her vibrance again. When Mama Vivian was alive, the two women were often teased for their sisterly bickering. They were decades apart in age, and their comrades could count on them to have very different perspectives on every single issue—even when they agreed on the fundamentals. Dune knew that Mama Vivian had respected Hoka; her grandmother had shared stories of how her family in China had lived under Japanese occupation, and how it was important to her that she and Hoka reject the colonial erasure of the word *Asian* and deal with the complex differences in the governance, economy, and culture of their homelands, the war residue in their intersections.

Dune had asked to speak with Hoka because she wanted to find a way off the Mbongi Council without disrespecting anyone or seeming to shirk her responsibility. They were side by side on the Riverwalk, Murmur City on their right, the Detroit River on their left, halved by the wall of vines that moved with the water but never enough for them to see the Canada side. The sun was directly above, and Dune noticed how her shadow was so tiny, directly below her.

"I don't know if I am cut out for . . . being like, a leader," Dune spoke softly. "Not like I need a pep talk; I just don't know if it's for me. The meetings."

With the sun above, it was almost warm enough to take off their jackets, but the wind across the water was decidedly cool. The wall, and the city it contained, were more beautiful each day. Dune always felt a slight disorientation looking at their border—as if she were looking down on a region of the northwest from a plane. They kept walking quietly until Hoka made a little *mmm* noise in her throat. Dune understood that this meant her elder wanted her to deepen the inquiry.

"Something about sitting in those spaces—it reminds me of being a child. I always thought it was because when I was a kid I didn't like the meetings. But now I'm grown and it still feels like I am faking it." Dune felt an unexpected sharpness at her eyes and shook her head, as if she could shake away the presence of her pain.

"Everyone's faking it, Dune." Hoka smirked at Dune without turning toward her. "At least at first, at least a little bit. We don't know what we are doing. That's why we talk so much about each thing, over and over. We are trying to make meaning in a world that is always changing. Trying to build justice out of sand. We'll never know."

"So then . . . how do you know it's, like, the right use of your time? Like, I feel like I could be gardening, or working with Mama Rue and that might be more useful."

"It might be. Only you can determine that."

"I just feel like people are fighting over silly things in there, like making everything into a little war. It doesn't need to be so difficult." Dune wanted Hoka to give her permission to go.

"There are people in there who have a very, very clear sense of what the future should look like. And in those visions of the next world, no one behaves like we do now. So, the frustration you feel—and I am not immune to it myself—this frustration is one of feeling the theoretical crowding into the space of the material."

Dune nodded. That was exactly it. "Like, people came to Murmur City to survive. We are surviving. I feel like the council could just focus on the acts of survival and we would be doing enough. But like, people want to make it about all this other shit. Why? There's nothing to argue about, we are surviving."

"Well, that's one way to see it," Hoka was skillful at disagreeing while staying connected. "The way I was trained, you are on the side of order or on the side of chaos. Anyone who says there are other options is trying to keep you dumb, to pull you into the chaos." Hoka's hands seemed to yank an invisible rope, to no avail. "In the chaos, everyone goes hungry. It looks like freedom, but freedom actually comes from stability, order, authentic agreements." Now her hands smoothed out, creating a line out ahead, a steady horizon. "Order. When there is order, we can take care of everyone. This place that we have carved out, this survival that we have grabbed onto, it is fragile, but it is not a place of chaos. If we do our work well, the order works so well that we are bored, and then we can make art and invent new wonders. And the order doesn't come from one mind, or one type of mind—that's a different chaos, authoritarian and frightening. This is the order we shape together. What is happening under the surface in those meetings is that everyone is figuring out how to maintain and sustain the order. We don't have a military, we don't have police—we have the Council. We only have order."

Now Hoka's hands seemed to be precisely placing parts of the world in place. "Every need is met. For almost three years we've been able to say that, and mean it. This is an astounding feat. For many of us in that room, this simple act of meeting and handling the things that come up, and seeking the best way to handle these things, this is us practicing the order that allows us freedom from dominant structures."

Dune felt the resistance in her.

"We are interested in this experiment, of holding the governance of Murmur City. But that doesn't mean *you* have to be. You are not Brendon, you are not Kama, they were policy nerds. You are Dune. You are deeply valuable to us in ways that they would never have imagined. But your contribution doesn't have to be through the council. If you want to step down, might I suggest you think of a few people who would be good replacements and let's have that conversation."

Dune felt immense relief flood her system. She smiled at Hoka and the elder wiggled her eyebrows a bit, celebrating the clarity of direction written all over Dune's face.

"And ... I know Dawud knows this, but I don't know if you do, if you've been over there ... but Murmur City isn't the only experiment." Hoka started walking again, so Dune moved to catch up.

"You mean like the farmers around the city?"

"No, most of them are part of Murmur City now, remote hubs of this place, this system. But there are a bunch of people living in 1300 Lafayette. Some people have migrated over there from here. They don't have the same arrangements as us, they don't see themselves as a part of Murmur City. But they do seem to work together to live, they're gardening on the roof and made their pool swimmable this summer. There are thirty floors in that building, a whole other ecosystem. Maybe *they* need you, and Rue, and magic?"

Dune was quiet; wondering what Dawud knew, why Hoka had mentioned it, not wanting to show Hoka how it felt to learn about 1300 Lafayette from her, wondering if Dawud hadn't told her on purpose. Hoka kept her eyes on the river as they reached the end of the walk and turned into the wind, back toward Murmur City. She added, "But maybe that's just a different kind of order."

Dune's Ancestor Journal, September

i have a broken heart. i think that's how i got here. i was fine i think, but i couldn't recover my heart, couldn't get it back in one big soft pounding place.

i knew it could be broken. i thought i knew what broken meant—i thought broken meant i could recover. i stood there thinking i would recover. i still think maybe i will recover.

but i don't know if i have a heart anymore—if i have all the pieces anymore. maybe a heart only works with a container to beat against.

detroit is only a dream to those with scorpio placements—for the rest of us this dirt breaks our hearts.

Listen

Dune was frustrated. "I just want to understand what this is, what I'm doing."

She was behind Mama Rue in the hallway, carrying the elder's bags, on their way back from a session where Mama Rue had seemed to do some kind of exorcism on a woman named Tressa who wouldn't get out of bed. Tressa's mother had asked Mama Rue to come. Tressa was in a room with blankets over the window and the room had smelled like something was rotting inside the walls. Mama Rue had pulled down the blankets to let the sun in and cranked up the AC. As cool air poured in, the thick stench poured out. They were able to clear some shadow from Tressa and Dune wanted to understand how.

"You're helping people."

Mama Rue was moving now with a bit of weave in her step, as she often did after their work, "so the spirits can't easily follow." She had called on Dune to sing something for Tressa, but no song came. Dune had scrambled inside herself for something else and started singing, "I don't know how my mother walked her trouble down," the opening of a medicine song called "I Remember, I Believe" from Sweet Honey in the Rock, but Mama Rue had given her a look that shut her up.

Mama Rue had gone straight to Tressa's head and held it. Her hands had created some kind of pressure in Tressa, and the woman had bucked in the bed, trying to get away from Mama Rue. But the elder was strong, and grounded, and she had made her own kind of howling wail. Dune had felt lost in the room.

"You talk to the ancestors! Directly!" Mama Rue blurted out, spinning in the hallway long enough to yell before dancing along.

Dune fumbled for an argument. She didn't feel like she was in any kind of coherent conversation with the ancestors, as much as she wanted to be.

"They are thick all around us, trying to help us, but *you* can hear them. You can make them hear you. This usually takes years of study and even then, the translations are rarely so pure from need into fulfillment. It must be because the ancestors are all so current, we are still in the same war."

Dune could see Mama Rue turning inwards in her thinking and tried to ask a question that would pull her back.

"But I don't know how to do it." Dune hitched one of the bags up on her shoulder. They were at Mama Rue's door now.

"Oh! Was that toy Detroit your wand?"

Dune's mind raced back to the basement of her parents' house, where her father had recreated Detroit. That model of the city had been where she mapped the death H-8 brought to the city. It had been the quiet place where she realized something magical was unfolding. But the magic that created the wall that now surrounded them had consumed the basement, and then the whole house. Mama Rue turned and searched Dune's face, grabbed her left hand and opened it, then looked back into Dune's eyes. "Can you talk to them without it?"

"I don't know! Maybe the journaling? But that just happens ... I haven't really tried."

"Well, try, fool girl! You are gifted but still so slow. The way you do your work is like watching someone fly against their own will . . . but you're not the first winged creature I've encountered. You're not the first channel to open. You're not the first of anything. You are not the only of anything. You are the one right now in this place, in this moment, and if you do not accept your role then maybe we die, or maybe someone else gets room to try, or maybe something I can't imagine happens. Don't get too caught up in the *you* of it all. Why you? Who cares, that's not the point. The point is right now you're open and available and life is coming through. Think. A lot of women can get pregnant and when you're pregnant you get that goddess glow, but that doesn't mean you are eternally anointed. You might be a shitty mom; I certainly had one of those and, honey, they *exist*. That don't make me less holy and my holiness don't make me better than nobody else. That's the trick of it all. That's the god of it all. Right now, you are the only one who can know what your magic . . . needs."

Dune set down the bags in frustration, rough enough that things in the bags jangled and banged around. She almost stomped off. "Everyone thinks I know, but I don't! I don't know how I did it. And I don't know how to keep doing it."

Mama Rue started opening her door. Dune felt desperate, but there was nothing else to say. The elder paused and shook her head as if the act of communicating in this pedestrian way, speaking aloud, was offensive to her.

"You didn't do it alone. The ones who helped you? They *know* you don't know. But they helped you and they can help you again, if you let them. If you ask for help. The model wasn't the breadth of your magic. You are. Figure out how to listen."

Mama Rue looked at Dune and clapped her hands hard, once.

Dune suddenly heard a thunderous cacophony, as if she were surrounded by a crowd. She closed her eyes, pulled in, trying to hear anything direct, or specific, in the roar. There was too much—too many sounds, too many voices, too many directions of attention and energy. Just at the moment when she was going to cry out in overwhelm, Mama Rue clapped again.

She stepped over to Dune and pulled her into a hug as surprising as it was necessary. She could feel the strength flowing through Mama Rue's arms, and then heard the elder whispering into her ear, "That's how I listen. You have a different way. Find yours."

Part 2

Fall, Compost

Over My Shoulder

Dune's Ancestor Journal, October
if life is trauma we don't have to stay, this isn't the only option
the living world is made from the dead on every level
which is why we can find recognizable silhouettes of life forms in all matter
soften your eyes when you look at the world and you see through time
maybe we can slip out of the pain
become a part of the world that no one can shatter

Homegoing

Dune wasn't consciously avoiding the house in which her whole life had happened. It wasn't an intentional thing. She just got busy and now she hadn't been back to the house in so long that she couldn't remember the last time. Life in Murmur City was full and when she left the world they were building there, it was usually with specific purpose, with places to go that didn't require driving up that short, dramatically wide segment of 2nd Avenue where she had learned to ride a bike, skateboard, and smoke weed.

Mama Rue had disrupted Dune's sense of self, first by calling her into this urgent, deep work with a kind of faith that Dune could do it, then by holding her accountable for what she couldn't do. And now by this suggestion of a wand, this suggestion that it was all collaboration, that both the material and the spirit of that house were part of the magic.

Dune leaned back on her bike, one foot on the corner curb where 2nd Avenue stretched from MLK Jr Boulevard up to Warren Ave, the southern border of the Wayne State campus. Dog panted at her side. For her entire life, the stretch had been open and clear, with the Fisher building visible up past the campus. Now, the road was blocked.

Dune looked at Dog, who was patiently waiting for her, poised to go explore as soon as she moved an inch. She pushed off and he ran, up the road full of tree. On the lot where her house had stood, and the street in front of it, there was now one of the most beautiful, robust trees Dune had ever seen, a tree that felt at least half a century old. Wide, low branches touched the road, grew into the nearby apartment buildings. The branches fingered the ruined top floor of Captain's house, which Dune had magicked across the street in a dream when her powers were first awakening.

Climate change meant summer was dragging itself out later and later each year, what Kama had called the "golden age of global warming." In Dune's childhood, any tree in October would have already been halfway done undressing its leaves. This tree, the whole block, felt full of life. The green leaves were dappled with gingko gold, an early fall palette that had always calmed her system. All around the trunk and wrapped around the branches were the vines that Dune knew also grew up the edges of the city. This tree grew from the same source that held up the wall. Others understood the preciousness of this tree. There were all kinds of offerings amongst the roots that reached out from the trunk: fresh and desiccated flowers, worn books, water mutated photos, stained stuffed animals. It was an altar. There were a few people leaning against the trunk, or sitting in the lower branches, quiet. The tree was so humongous that they were each in their own experience. Dog moved around them discreetly as he explored the smells of the tree. Dune understood that for him this was a familiar place.

And there was a door, up in the branches.

Dune laid her bike on the ground, awestruck. Near the door a broom-head jutted out of a branch, and a bit further down Mama Vivian's chair with the blanket still draped over the back lay in a junction of branches. With her eyes refocusing to look for home, she scanned the tree. The bark, the trunk, was full of the house, chunks of the pale-yellow outer walls here, a bathtub that remembered being white grown vertical there, even brief patterns where Kama's clothes had been swallowed, integrated into this being. Dune walked up to the massive trunk that grew right through the road. Reaching out, still a foot away, she could feel the life force of the tree pulsing.

When she laid her palms against the bark, she had to close her eyes because she could see her old kitchen so clearly. She saw the sun falling through the small window, she felt how crowded it was, she saw her own hands on the oak table.

The oak table.

Kama's oak table had recovered from the wound that made it into a table. It had recovered exponentially.

Dune was in tree time, for a long time, feeling how this oak reached down and out, weaving roots into trees around it. She could feel that somewhere at the center of this structure there was still a small table full of Detroit's dead, a sacred catacomb at the heart of the tree. She could feel that the tree was lonely, and hardworking. That it kept growing because it wanted to be close to others, which was hard to do as a tree in the middle of a city.

The tree had so much to tell her.

When she opened her eyes it was dusk. The other visitors were gone. Dog was sitting a ways behind her, facing away from her. She loved his protective nature. She felt only love pouring in and out of her. She stepped away from the tree, rooted. When she reached Dog, she saw that he had an elegant length of fallen branch in front of him. He looked at it and at her a few times, so she knew it was an offer. She picked it up and tied it into her bike basket with a little bungee cord, beaming her gratitude at Dog.

Now, she had a wand.

Dune's Ancestor Journal, October

the ancestors are always there, always with you. when you don't ask for their support, they grow heavy, forgotten. when you call on them, on your benevolent ancestors, their memory self can activate on your behalf. their souls are at peace, but everything in the universe has particle existence as memory in every moment and every place and everyone they connect to in life. memory, dark matter, it is the unseen thickness of existence. it is the river of energy moving forward toward the not-yet-known, in your body.

Dune set the wand on the windowsill. Dawud had shown her

how to carve it, and she had done the bare minimum to make it something she could easily hold in her hand. It became her altar —anywhere she set it down became an intentional ritual space. The wood that had grown through the dirt, drunk the rain and withstood the wind, all powered by the fire of the sun. She now understood that she was listening to the dead in those dark, early morning hours, and the wand made the sacred connection feel safe. Dune would wake up, hearing something like a voice in her head, often with a rhythm to it. She would pad over to the windowsill altar and write down whatever she heard, as precisely as possible, then crawl back into bed for more sleep.

Drive

Dawud was rubbing Dune's feet and calves when she woke up, and she had no idea how long he'd been doing it. She stretched long in the bed, pressing into his hands as she looked at him. She could tell he had a plan for the day and it showed in his shoulders, in the neutral set of his mouth.

Their bed was piles and piles of pillows, blankets, sheets. It felt more like an adult fort than a sensible bed. Both of them had gotten wilder and wilder in their dreaming, finding more and more places that needed the support of another pillow. They had evolved a practice of holding each other when they slept, starting as a full cuddle and then cooling into holding hands, or Dawud's hand on Dune's back, or her hand on his ass.

They kept the bedroom shadowy and each side of the bed was a clear representation of the differences between them. On Dune's side there were books, open magazines, neat stacks based on where she was in the process of learning. On Dawud's side were the clothing items he was wearing that week, a choice of shirts, pants, and socks that had only been worn once and were definitely going to get two to three more wears. He had multiple water bottles, tech that needed charging, and half-empty mugs, which always made Dune feel a little flutter of father-grief.

Their whole space had this duality; they each had a side of the dining room table, they each had a counter in the kitchen, they each had a sink in the bathroom, an end of the shower, a worn spot on the couch. They were still wildly distinct; their living together was an act of parallels more than integration. And Dawud often woke up with plans, while Dune woke up crawling deeper into the covers.

"And what are we doing?" Dune's morning voice was playful.

"It's my birthday."

Dune sat up. They had both been secretive and understated about their birthdays. In the initial crisis world of H-8 it hadn't mattered, and then it'd felt too pedestrian to ask.

"Stay calm," he kept his hands on her in a grounding way. "I want to do something that might be fun or unfun. I just want to do it with you."

Dune tried to match his cool, but everything in her wanted to geek out about this offer, this intimate invitation. She settled on keeping her face straight while doing a little shoulder shimmy. Dawud gave her an eyebrow and then started shimmying with her.

"You ready?"

Dune was in her home uniform, a sports bra and boxers. She made the face at him, the one that meant "wow you really love me if you think this would be suitable to wear outside." Dawud pulled her up against him, squeezing her in as many places as he could reach. Dune was soft with him, a softness she had never known she could enjoy. She liked spilling over his hands. He started kissing on her neck, but caught her hands as she pulled at the band of his sweatpants.

"Later, I want all of that. But first I want to show you some things."

Dune was surprised. Dawud was generally always available for a quickie, for something. But his voice was soft and he was steady, and she considered that perhaps there was something more intimate than sex that he wanted to give her. Based on his layers, they were going to be outside. She got up and met his quiet, changing into outside clothes, layering up until she matched him.

Dawud led her down into the parking garage, which had a few of their vehicles mixed in amongst the thousands that had been left behind in the evacuation—only the electric ones were usable now that no gas was coming into the city. Dawud's current favorite was a Mustang Mach-E SUV in an outrageous shade of orange with fire patterns along both sides. It was an absolutely ridiculous car, too dangerously bright for a Black man to drive in America; in this new, unsupervised Detroit, he could drive it with music blasting.

Dune scooted ahead enough to open the driver's side door for Dawud, eliciting a spank from him.

He got in the car and immediately pulled out a CD with "Ocean Drive" written in block print, above a bunch of smaller writing in sharpie. Dune didn't know the vehicle even had a way to play CDs, but Dawud had a whole set-up that fed into the system. She could feel that the CD was a crucial part of the experience. The first song came on: "My Girl" by The Temptations. She appreciated the layers of their relationship, that she could enjoy the song without feeling possessed or girlish. They both knew Dawud was the sunshine and she was the cloudy day.

They were driving east on Jefferson, the river and the wall to their right. The music combined with the daylight spilling through the sunroof and Dawud's overt pleasure. Dune felt at ease. Eventually he turned left on Cadieux Road. He pulled to a stop in front of a strange cream-colored mid-century home that had abstract red and blue bricks sparsely positioned on the front. She wanted to go inside.

"Other way, baby."

She looked away from the house and there was a hospital, the lot's entrance chained closed. Beaumont Hospital. Dune looked at Dawud and he smiled, childlike—Dune had a moment of dream déjà vu, seeing snapshots of him as a child and a man all at once.

"This is where I was born, nine days ahead of schedule. My mother thought that where I was born would shape where I could go to school." Dawud wasn't joking. Dune asked the question with her eyebrows. "It didn't."

He got back on the highway and turned the music back on. Marvin Gaye was singing "Stubborn Kind of Fellow." Dune felt a growing energy in Dawud, unspoken memories spiraling out from him to fill the car with nostalgia. This journey was very important to him.

The front of the red brick building they pulled up to next was his elementary school, Rosa Parks Academy. It looked very square and contained and like it would have maybe held four classrooms inside. Intimate. There was a small playground fenced in on the right side of the building, along with some overgrown plant beds. He parked in front and stepped out. Dune followed him into the brisk fall air. It looked like it was going to rain by nightfall, but that was just the sky this time of year.

"I was always a little smart for my age. Not smart enough to skip grades, but enough to bother everyone around me when I was bored. I would get a question in my head that had nothing to do with the topic at hand, and just have to follow it until I understood. They would sit me in a corner or send me outside to work the energy out in the cold."

They circled the school before climbing back in the car. Mary Wells was singing "The One Who Really Loves You." He turned onto Livernois, "one of my all-time favorite street names," to show her a piece of fresh graffiti on an underpass. He would neither admit nor deny this was his work, but he looked proud when they pulled up. In purple block letters, it read:

WHOEVER SURVIVES HAS TO REMEMBER THE WONDER

Next stop, Cass Tech. "That isn't actually the building. It was there," he pointed just south of the structure they'd parked in front of, which was all stacked levels of greenish glass and brick red. Dune didn't remember when the old building burned down, but she was pretty sure Kama had brought her to watch as a child, and she remembered when they had finally torn it down. She kept this to herself, tuning into Dawud's story. "By this point, they wanted to hold me back because I skipped class so much. I was losing my shit, trying to be the man of the house. I was on the football team, I could kick and I could throw, couldn't tackle shit. And I knew, without any confusion, that I wanted to fuck *everyone* on the team, and that if I said so to anyone, they would probably kill me in a lot of horrible torturous ways. Instant bad. I skipped class, smoked cigarettes, and found this super nerdy Black boy, he didn't talk a lot, but we touched each other."

Dune couldn't look away from Dawud, his eyes so soft and clearly looking through time.

"He was beautiful. Behind his glasses, his eyes were . . . windows. Beautiful. His mouth was lush. He seemed scrawny with clothes on, but naked, he looked like a sculpture. He was born with six fingers on both hands, and they did surgery to remove the extra digits when he was a kid so his hands were really unique. He was so fucking smart . . . He would bring poems, like read me poems. Like no context," Dawud laughed. "These folded up poems in his back pocket. He would read it and look at me like it made everything make more sense."

Dawud was quiet, in his memory for a minute. Shaking his head. "Hello Stranger" by Barbara Lewis began to play.

"Anyway, he died, my senior year." Dawud was struggling to speak. Dune's first instinct was to look away, to give him some kind of privacy even as she reached over and placed her hand on his arm. For a half second, as she turned her head away from him, she knew that the vehicle was surrounded by a circle of praying people. But they were on a wide open, empty, gray 2nd Avenue. She shook the vision away and poured her love through her hand into him.

"For two years he was the person I touched, like the only person I touched that wasn't on a field or in a fight. We took each other's virginity. He would hold me, just for a few minutes after. I walked around with him on my mind and in my body. And then he fucking—he died by suicide, day before my seventeenth birthday. And no one even knew that I *knew* him. Like, I had to listen to everyone talk about him, my beloved teammates calling him a 'faggot,' saying that he did the only logical thing for a 'shit-dick ass eater.'"

Dawud's fingers moved just slightly in front of him to quote the vile language of hate, place it at some small distance from his own heart. He looked at her then, briefly. "His name was Richard. He was my first love."

"I'm so sorry for that loss. And that you had to grieve in secret." Dune risked moving her hand up to his shoulder. He collapsed against her touch, grabbing her hand and pressing it against his forehead as he wept. She pulled him against her shoulder and got soft, intuiting that the energy could flow through her and out. Time passed, marked by his breath moving in and out of the torrent. When he spoke again it was a quiet, steady Dawud that she'd never heard before.

"Shit was so dangerous, babe. Like, I *had* to be aroused by the taboo of it all. I had to develop all these faces and voices, none of them really me. I had to survive, with no one to hold me. When I found out about the National Guard, about a way out of here, a way to be a man that no one would question . . ."

Dawud shook his head. "For years, I found men who would fuck me. That was easy. But it's been hard finding men to hold me. Or, if they would hold me, they wanted to get married or act like we were. They wanted my freedom. Richard just wanted to hold me."

After a while beached on her shoulder, Dawud sat up, cleared his throat, and began the drive to their next destination. They drove quietly, Dune's hand on his thigh. She felt worlds between them, conversations of possession and ownership and freedom and marriage and commitment and love and lust, all touched but somehow unexamined, as if everyone would lose something precious if they said what they really did and didn't want.

He pulled them into the round driveway of 1300 Lafayette, the mid-century high-rise apartment building Hoka had mentioned.

Dawud parked haphazardly there, in front of a revolving door that was once clearly monitored by a doorman. Dune had never actually been inside the building—it was for older people, people who could buy an apartment. She felt dread, quick and shadowy.

He held her hand so they squeezed through the rotating door together. There was a Black man sitting inside, supine, reading a magazine on a round couch. It wasn't until he and Dawud nodded at each other that Dune realized the guy was a security guard.

Dawud dipped behind the desk and pushed some buttons. "Calling the elevator."

Then he took her hand and guided her to the elevator bank. Elevator B arrived almost immediately. A small screen on the wall announced that the elevator was bound for the ninth floor; there were no buttons anywhere inside to direct the machine.

On the ninth floor he guided her to the end of the hallway, to an apartment with no numbers or letters on it. Dune kept an eye on him and an eye on the world around them. He opened the door onto a short hallway, a mirrored closet on their right. He flipped a switch and walked her in, turning to the left. The hall opened onto an empty room, one entire wall made of windows, overlooking their city.

Dune felt the clear line of dread move through her. This stop on Dawud's tour wasn't about his past. It was somehow going to change her future.

"Did a lover live here?" She asked, dishonest in her question, wanting to make some other thing true.

"Not yet."

Dune's gut washed cold.

She walked up to the window, pressing her hands against it, seeing how much of the city sprawled from here to the far-off boundary, her wall. He'd met someone more free-spirited than her, someone with a big girthy organic penis, someone . . . else. And she had to be ok with it. She tried to keep her face neutral.

Dawud was right behind her. He placed his hands over hers, on the glass. "Turn around."

She slid her hands out from his and turned in the tight cage of his arms, confused. He saw something in her face that made a soft smile of concern arrive on his. "This is our second home, if you like it." Between them, Dune's laughter spilled the fear out of her; she was truly surprised. "I need a place away from Murmur City, I need something a bit more chaotic and collective and wild. Nobody here expects anything from anyone else. They all chip in to feed the guards and it's fucking chill. And before you say yes, I would like to christen it with my birthday blow job."

Before he could ask any questions, gain any clues on where she had traversed in her inner loop, how she had lost him, accepted the loss, seen the story of her life feeling forever lonely without him, she kissed him. Her mouth was sloppy around his bottom lip, teasing him with what was coming. She began to slide down to her knees, but he caught her, "No, no. One second."

He slipped back into the hallway, then rolled in with a step stool and positioned it right in front of the window. She sat on it and adjusted the height lower, until she could rest her head back against the glass and take him. She began singing, slow and throaty.

"Happy birthday to ya . . ."

Completions

Marta

November 7, 2029

Dear Dune,

I am sorry. I am sorry.

I am sorry for cheating on us.

I am sorry for messing up the possibilities of our love.

I am sorry for not getting my shit together when I had you.

I am sorry for leaving you in Detroit. I should have stayed, I think.

I am sorry for always making everything about me—I tried to write this so it wasn't I I I, but I had to say I'm sorry so hopefully you get that.

Please forgive me.

Please respond.

I want to come home. Is that possible? They say it's not possible to enter, but maybe you know a way.

Dune, please. Please. Please.
I'm sorry.
With love forever, not a bot or a fed,
Marta

Dune's Ancestor Journal, November

in some ways we are kama, recognizable to you, to my child, to our community, to myself. but in other, very important ways, we are that which always existed and will always exist, which flowed briefly thru kama's life. the storyteller who does not know the ending. and this is going to feel familiar and foreign to you because you so thoroughly identify with yourself and your current container of life, but you also feel the otherness in you. the before and after, the question about what really matters.

justice at the scale of one life does matter. we are certain of it. we can tell you from here that each life can fill the space of all life at any given moment. and the spirit of the universe is fickle and interested. any life can become important, if not in the way it is lived, then in the way it dies.

the way we died made my life important to strangers; the way we lived made it important to the people who knew me, loved me, came to life thru my body. there are people who say about me that we changed their lives and i believe them, that crossing our path redirected theirs. it's all less direct than we imagine, even when it looks like cause and effect. there are so many people who have opinions about my death, experts on my condition who never once touched my skin. the people who examined me, looking for the cause of my silence, found my broken heart everywhere, it wasn't even in my chest anymore. our system was devoid of serotonin, empty of anything that could help me see a reason to live. this was a chemical dishonesty. we wanted to live. we wanted everyone in the world to want to live, to have lives good enough to want them.

i failed at this mission in my life. if we cannot get dune to hear us, i will fail this mission in death.

Dune's Role

Since Dune's talk with Hoka, she had been unsure about her role on the Mbongi Council, attending meetings but not engaging much, feeling herself in a kind of holding pattern. Was Hoka going to find a way for Dune to get out of this? Unclear. The elder had given Dune no particular kind of attention, and now it was November.

"Today I would like to add a membership question," Hoka said as they were reviewing the agenda, the only other item on it to revisit a now-annual conversation on whether a city where one-fifth of the population was non-Black could qualify as a maroon space.

"What membership question?" asked Mama Tazina.

"Dune."

Everyone looked at Dune as she tried to also somehow look at herself. She gave a small smile, not wanting to look too eager. She was glad Hoka had said this now, as it would surely become the immediate topic of conversation. Then it occurred to her she might have to say something, and her stomach flipped.

"What exactly is the question?" Mohamed followed. He looked curious, one of his two default settings. The other was suspicion, but Dune felt none of that as he looked at her.

"Well, she isn't a meeting person, but she has a lot to offer the community through her magical practice." Hoka made the spell work feel practical, like gardening, like janitorial services. "And there is a piece of work we desperately need done, which I think she might be perfect for."

Dune could feel the eyes on her and hoped they could all see that she had no idea what Hoka was talking about; she stopped just short of pantomiming cluelessness.

"For nearly three years we have been living in a community where people have a variety of magical powers, and we haven't inventoried them, we haven't asked anyone what they can do. We know, if the powers are obvious, if people volunteer themselves to do something, if we witness. But shouldn't we *know*? Isn't this an untapped resource? Shouldn't we begin an earnest assessment of the powers that have persisted?" As Hoka spoke, Dune's mouth nearly watered. The general understanding was that, after the initial wave of H-8 deaths, a lot of the powers people had come into had muted or disappeared, but to her knowledge no one had really been tracking it.

The group murmured. Dune stayed quiet.

"Would she still be a part of this council?" Mama Tazina asked the room.

Hoka looked at Dune, the slightest amusement on her lips. "Yes, but in a liaison-type role. Dune, what I would like to ask you to do is map the magic of Murmur City. First come up with a process to gather and map the data—work with Mohamed's team on securing the data if that feels necessary. And then we, as a council, can talk about application. Like, are there certain kinds of magic that should be deputized into certain kinds of work? And how to do that while protecting free will?"

The council erupted in questions and thoughts, and Hoka threw her hands up to pause it. "Dune, can you come back to us next week with a proposal on how this could work? And if people have ideas, can they bring them to you?"

Dune was already nodding. "Yes—I'll stay after the meeting today to hear any input you guys have, and . . . yeah."

The meeting moved on, and Dune sat there, buzzing in her belly with ideas.

After they formally adjourned, Mohamed came over and sat with Dune. At first he was sharing with her different collections of data he thought might be useful to her—maps of where people lived outside Murmur City in case she wanted to cross examine the data, hours when she could come to the observatory and view footage of magical acts they'd documented for posterity.

"It's really quite something, isn't it, that our magic has been less interesting than our survival," his voice was familiar to her now, lilting, Southern, and soft. His face always reached for the stoic, even when he was smiling. Mohamed's family had fled from Beirut, Lebanon, to Birmingham, Alabama, when he was a child. For a long time, he and his parents and siblings had been the only non-locals, much less Arabs, in their neighborhood. He learned English with a drawl.

"Yeah, I feel like I haven't really had time to learn what I can still do. I want to understand it. And I bet I'm not the only one."

"Dune," Mohamed looked around, triple checking that they were alone. Confirming that, he lowered his voice even further. "When you sit with the maps and the numbers, you'll see this, so I will share it with you now. There are a lot more people here, in Detroit. Part of . . . One of the kinds of magic is a kind of obscuring presence. A lot of my people, people from Lebanon, Palestine, Syria, Turkey—the magic we know is how to live in a place where no one wants us to live. We all have a sprinkling of this magic."

What he was telling her had the feeling of a glass bird—she didn't know how to look at it *and* hold it safely. "They're still in Dearborn?" she asked, her mind mapping out where the wall was the last time she'd driven out that way.

"Some. So many of us have been displaced too many times. They were offered home here and said no thank you." Mohamed smiled, both of and outside his people as he spoke. "I think their magic might be very, very important to learn about."

"I agree," Dune matched his somber energy. She would keep his secret. She wondered just how many people were stolen away on this ship of land moving through time.

Dune's Ancestor Journal, November

Most of the time, when Dune heard ancestors talking, it was a monologue, a download, like she was hearing someone speak in another room. Since she had started journaling, she listened most mornings for ancestor voices. At first, she'd thought it was something that came to her, but slowly she was understanding it was more like the Detroit River. The river was always flowing, even under winter's ice. If you went to it, you could almost always scoop up some water. The ancestors were always communicating, available. If she went with a clear mind, she would always hear *something*, even if it wasn't exactly what she had aimed for. She was always aiming for Kama, or Brendon, or Elouise. One of her known ancestors, one of her new ancestors.

It was daunting the first time she heard more than one voice. It was still one voice, but one voice explicitly trying to speak as two people. It was Kama, trying to gossip about a conversation with Brendon. It took Dune a while to even figure out how to write it down, she landed on scribbled hearsay. It felt hard to understand in a way that made her miss her mother more than ever.

he said: you made a portal. to another place. detroit, not that much different, but here Black people are loved by themselves and everyone else.

and i was so quick and sharp: that's it? and that's only possible in a parallel world?

and he said: I'm just saying what you did with the poison.

so i killed us?

he said: oh, no ... i'm dead. and ok with it. you're in some other kind of place. maroon space.

i begged him: you're in between. if you can reach me you can reach her.

but he said this is truer for me than for him.

i want to enjoy being reunited with him, but there is something more important—i need to reach our child, i need to help her, protect her, guide her ... i need to apologize for leaving her.

he says i am not in control of any of that, or anything else. and that once i accept that, i can go with him.

the others came with me, why won't she? ... she still has hope in her life, her body, her possibility.

why is she trying to do this alone? my child ...

After the transmission, Dune flooded with doubt. Was this a download or a dream? Was Dune having a fantasy where her parents longed for her as she longed for them? Was she actually hearing them? She could believe every other ancestor voice ... but her own parents? And did Kama want her to die? Did Kama not know she herself was dead? What was the portal? Was her mother wrong, or was this like life, where Dune had been the last to understand her mother's wisdom?

Captain

When Captain was ready to die, he said so.

He asked Dune for a family dinner. She brought a somewhat tense Dawud and a playful Jizo with their plates and glasses. They sat around the square card table and Captain began to talk, a smile growing on his face. He glowed in the way that Black men who make it to old age glow; improbable, victorious.

"Like I told Miss Dune over here, I have reached the end of my very good life. Naw, don't act like that, not when I got this whole bonus chapter with y'all.

"Jizo, you stay good, you got a good heart, and you might be a angel or a saint but you deserve to live your own life now. Thank you for giving me such good days."

Jizo stood up and ran around the table to hug Captain and kiss his soft, ancient cheeks, pouring love from his eyes. The child was always making little rituals. Dawud and Dune looked at each other, both holding a good cry in their faces.

"Dawud, you a stand-up man. You a real good man, coming back here to do this with us. You keep your wits about you—I promise you there ain't nothing better out there, I know you gotta learn that yourself."

Dawud laughed and raised himself from his seat enough to kiss Captain on the forehead. "Thank you, sensei." As he sat down, tears shone in his eyes, spilling when he blinked.

"And you," Captain tilted his head and attention to Dune, "you've done some things I don't really understand. But that's alright with me, supergirl. I just want to say, everyone can take care of themselves now. You done enough. You can rest, ok?"

Dune sucked her teeth, rolled her eyes, to keep her face together. Then she grabbed Captain's hand and smiled at him, tears coming softly over her cheeks.

"Ok then. I'm going to be with Delilah."

Captain turned towards the window, surveying the city as if imprinting it in his mind forever. Then he closed his eyes, sat back, and exhaled. He didn't inhale; Dune felt the life leave his hand in hers. "Oh! Captain!"

Then they were all holding him and letting him go.

Dog

The first man is gone, the old one who was always smiling, who lived with the spirit woman.

The people are crying for the old man and everyone else who is gone. They leave tears all over me and I take them to the river. I take them to the wood with no opening and howl them into the whole world.

Heavy

Dune's Ancestor Journal, November
right as i lay down to sleep, in the dark, *as i pivot to supine,* the dream i woke up from that very morning shows back up like an open portal full of details. sometimes there is just one feeling, one line. are these my dreams or *ancestral journeys*? this feeling, this question more than anything else makes me feel like i travel between worlds when i sleep, more than dream. but is any of this a dream now? this morning i woke with: *"i am always well rested and i feel delightful. i feel so full and i feel belonging. but oh, how i miss someone."*

Jizo
The night Captain died, Dune and Dawud set up a mattress in their living room for Jizo, and Dune sang him to sleep. Jizo seemed content, if a bit lost. He didn't seem saddened by Captain's death—if anything he seemed happy for his friend. Everyone

could feel Delilah's presence. She had lived with all of them for months, helping Captain to transition to her world.

The next day, Dawud found that Jizo's mattress was empty. Dune was in her own world of grief, in the bed watching icy damp wind move through the leaves outside the window. Dawud kept talking to her as if she was functional, so she grunted a few times to offer him some comfort. Dawud went out into Murmur City to search for Jizo in their normal places, but no one had seen him. He returned to Dune, this time truly needing her to think with him. Jizo was gone.

Dune was muted, "Why are you panicking?"

"He's a kid who just lost his caretaker. What if he's somewhere just scared as fuck?"

"He's fine." Dune pulled the covers back up over her shoulders.

"We don't know that—"

"I do." Dune snarked at Dawud. If she'd had fangs she would have bared them.

"How?" Dawud sat on the edge of the bed, placing a hand on Dune's hip. She closed her eyes for a moment.

"I can sense him." Her eyes were still closed, sifting inside herself. "I can't explain it exactly, but I can feel his life force. I can feel yours. I can feel . . ." Rio. "Everyone. If I think of people, I can feel them in here."

Dawud was nodding when Dune opened her eyes. In another circumstance, this would be a cool discovery. Right now, it just felt practical.

Jizo stayed away for three days. When Dawud and Dune woke up on the fourth day of grieving Captain, Jizo was sleeping in his bed, and he was a pre-teen. There was no soft transition, none of the normal years-long mutation from boy into young man. He'd grown at least seven inches, his soft small body suddenly long and lanky, massive long feet hanging off the end of the mattress. He still had an angel's soft puckered face, but now it lifted into blades of cheekbone, a shade shy of gaunt. His skin tone had deepened into a brown-olive. There was even a hint of acne across his forehead.

But it wasn't just his body. Jizo had a look on his face that they'd never seen—he seemed . . . annoyed.

Dune's Ancestor Journal, November

we remember brendon's voice. at first i thought i couldn't be attracted to him, when we heard his voice. it was so soft, so high. we had grown up with a certain kind of man around me, a voice that would be respected in a bar, in a factory, in the dark, in a household, regardless of the strength, power, economics, or capacity of the man using the voice. these men learned early to pitch their voices low, towards our listening bellies, rumbling intimately underground.

not brendon. his voice was obedient even in absence of instruction. it took us a while to understand when he was angry because he never got louder, just colder, quieter. his rage was a sharp arctic wind, rare and palpable—even if i was in a different room and he was calling out to me, we could tell when a fight was brewing in him. we fought calmly, making cases. when i would flare up he would hold his silence until i took a breath and met his eyes. he needed to know i was still me, recognizing him, even thru the anger.

this was a revelation, this had great appeal to me. we learned to be aroused by the sound of his voice, asking me what we wanted, what felt good to me, what bothered us, what shut us down.

the women in our line were strong, but that was only celebrated in the context of the care they gave their men. the women in my family carried the men, literally, emotionally, economically. love was the feeling of wanting to care for a man, that's what we were shown. when we met brendon, it was confusing. he was not interested in how we cared for him. he was interested in whether or not i cared about the ideas that were buzzing around in his head, making him feel lonely, like his mother had had all the thoughts and now there was nothing left but to live in them. he was excited when we appeared, together, to stumble on a new idea: that loving each other was itself a potentially radical act, not as a performance, but as an intimate practice of explicitly weaving culture. he thought, we thought, mama vivian would certainly be interested in this idea, which felt like a downstream idea of her concepts of community. and perhaps, if it hadn't been her son in a case study with me, she would have thrilled to it. but it was, he was, i was, we were, out of her control. and he still chose me.

she made it a competition and he chose us. here, though, there is somehow enough of him for both of us. enough of everything, really— time, space, things to attend to, or not, ease and support.

when someone dies violently, they become very powerful spirit allies to humans in their same condition. we are each other's saints. there is an eternity between revenge and justice, and some ancestors need all of that time to truly be able to help.

time is not heavy here, there is no torture to it. it is always now, all of it is now, now is always available. now, we are writing to you, helping you, in ceremony with you, watching you sleep. watching you have mediocre banter with a new lover while dreaming of more. feeling the small wounds of dehumanization open, soul spilling out of you in droplets. feeling the loneliness of surviving, listening to you complain, wishing you would ask for help.

right now it feels as though dune is rejecting my help in every now, but we are in no rush. i will be here when she calls me. we will be here if she doesn't call us, her witness.

The Weight

Dune's grief for Captain was numbing. She got high and didn't want to come down, ever. Didn't want to feel anything sharp ever again. Time was passing, but she was not passing it. She was sitting at her window while Dawud brought her meals and kept an eye on Jizo, who had moved back into the apartment he'd shared with Captain, self-sufficient in a way that was ageless. Dawud came and sat by her as well, and she wanted to comfort him, help him, or receive his help—but all she felt was drowning guilt for the selfishness of her grief, topped only by the desire to wallow on her own.

After a week, she told Dawud she needed a few days alone, totally alone. He loaded the fridge with food and took Jizo off to the Lafayette apartment.

That night, Dune ate so much she made herself sick, throwing up so hard she wet herself. She cleaned up, her shame quieting even her inner thoughts. She was almost asleep when the weight woke her up. It felt like someone was on the bed with her, though in the soft half-light of nighttime and charging electronics she could see there was no one there. She made the soft sounds she used to speak to Dog, who sometimes slept on a pillow on her floor. No Dog.

A shadow was slowly moving up her body.

The weight pressed the duvet down around her, over her feet, up her ankles. She had the clear thought that she should be afraid, but she was here and she could feel nothing sinister, just presence, palpable presence. A weight on her, of her. She didn't know where it came from or what it wanted. She knew she could bear the weight.

But the weight didn't need bearing. She realized as sleep came crawling back over her, this was a heft of comfort. She only wanted to lay here, under her ghosts.

Marta

Marta had slowly made her way north, careful in how she dressed, wearing baggy clothes and strategizing where she got gas based on the flags and signs in the area. The political conditions of the country could be simplified to the willfully ignorant vs the terrified frozen.

The willfully ignorant were working to turn back any protection of human rights; they had a chokehold on the state of Florida, where Marta and her parents had evacuated in the first rush of the virus. The terrified frozen were dissociated, struggling to find the courage to fight back, though they loved to point in terror at what was happening, show they understood it.

As a woman traveling alone, Marta was very aware that no matter what she wore, no matter how obedient she was to the law, she could be harassed, abducted, raped, or killed, and there would likely be no repercussions. If she got pregnant in most of the states she was journeying through, she would be detained until she birthed the baby. If the baby was born out of wedlock it would be seized as a "warden of the state." She kept her head down.

She had heard the news of the overgrowth around the city of Detroit reaching for the sky. She had seen the pictures of epic green where the skyline used to be. She knew that nothing went in or out or over, though she couldn't really understand how that was possible. She knew that if the government and military hadn't been able to get around the barrier, she probably wouldn't either. But she had made a mistake, left a beloved behind.

She thought of Dune every day, reliving and redoing their relationship, trying to learn everything she could, fantasizing about reuniting. She had tried dating new people, making friends, building community. But she had been raised amongst people who were neither ignorant nor frozen, and began to worry about what she would lose if she kept being in conversations with minds as limited in their imaginations as her Florida neighbors: weather, weather, racism, weather . . . never any questions. She longed for that Detroit sense of purpose, that ability to act. She needed to get back to the D, to see if Dune was somehow alive there, to see if the life she'd abandoned was still possible.

Every approach to Detroit is flat midwestern land; the only places that roll or elevate are highways moving through and around the massive factories and power plants that once supported nearly two million residents. When Marta left Detroit with her parents at the beginning of the plague, there were about half a million people who called Detroit home. Now she was driving along the gray emptiness of 75, the River Rouge plant and Zug Island filling her windows. The landscape on either side of her looked like the metallic apocalypse she'd been socialized to expect, but lifeless, no breath of smoke filling the sky. Normally this was the first place where she could see the Detroit skyline. What she saw instead made her hit the brakes.

There are many things in the world that can't be captured on film, despite effort and skill. Marta had found every news story about the natural barrier growing around Detroit, reading them with obsession, fear, and longing. One of her favorite feelings was original awe, the very first moment of seeing something truly astounding and holy. Something about scale, surprise, and the overlay of what is on top of what is expected means that often the first dumbstruck moment of awe can only be experienced, not documented.

Marta opened her car door and stepped out onto Highway 75, which for almost seventy years had ended at one of the busiest border crossing points in the country. Standing in the middle of this road any moment before this one would have been its own miracle, likely to get her killed or arrested. But now she stood alone, with the expanse of the wall before her.

For a moment her eyes and mind couldn't make sense of what she was seeing—it looked like an autumn forest was turned on its side, and the forest was growing towards her, reaching for her. Then her eyes shifted and she understood that the wall was reaching up, as if all of Detroit was a child wanting god to pick her up. The barrier was stunning—massive, but finite. She knew she could drive around all the parts of it that weren't in the Detroit River. It was thick, but she could sense light through it as well, especially closer to the top. That helped, to feel it truly was a wall with something held safely inside, not just a wild city-eating forest. Since it had grown, nothing was able to fly above it, no one was able to get a perspective into the world inside the wall.

Marta needed to get through that wall. She slowly drove closer, feeling an ominous twinge; it was so big, so mysterious. If the wall began to move in her direction, if she were swallowed up trying to go inside, no one would ever know. She hadn't told her parents where she was going, and no one could reach the people inside the city. If she was able to get through, it would be the same to her people as if she had evaporated.

Except she chose it. She didn't think of herself as suicidal;

moving towards the city was daunting, but it felt like there was a life worth living beyond the wall. She turned on to Southfield and drove up to the city's new perimeter as night fell.

Marta eventually slept in her car in a parking lot in Grosse Pointe. Just being this close to the city made her feel the comfort of Dune somehow.

Bitter

Dune found the music of her melancholy—Dinah Washington singing "This Bitter Earth"—and then turned it up because the room felt too big again. Dawud might not come back. She might never see him again. That was always a danger when they were apart; tonight it scared her, made her nauseous.

Ever since she had moved into Murmur City, she had thought it was too big; the windows stretched floor to ceiling, the light inescapable. Her rooms were on a curve that rolled from the river up the east side, Jefferson Ave stretching off to Grosse Pointe beyond the wild wall. What she could see was too much to look at all at once. A chill moved through her, a wave from her heart to her edges, so fast that she shuddered.

When Dawud was there, he was a consistent horizon. Watching his face could shift her day, listening to him laugh at shit happening in his head would relax her. The world was the soft space between the two of them; his solidity was her comfort.

But now he was gone, and her green wall was too far away and the sounds all seemed to echo in the space.

She missed him. She loved him.

And she was reminded of the delicious gift of deep solitude. Of having everything she needed, and a whole house to herself.

She remembered how differently she felt in her skin when she was naked without a witness. When there was no one else's desire to navigate and no one else to consider as she flowed through her day.

She felt a shift in her waking attention, a decline in the soft habitual turn towards him and his well-being, that subtle and even hidden pivot folded into her mind. She would not admit to herself that he had her attention in that way, but as he stayed away, she noticed the return of other waking thoughts, thoughts that weren't shaped by care, but by curiosity.

She found her impulses clearer, an energy to do something beyond Murmur City.

She returned to her own smell, which emerged when she wasn't showering in anticipation of daily sex. She smashed each of her lovers from her pores, her own salt forest scent re-emerging.

Dog
The human who laughs from the belly and the young elder went to the lonely tower. The human who grew the city can't stop crying. She doesn't even wipe her face. She fights the air, like there is pain in her chest or in her belly and she can't escape it but is still trying to crawl out of herself. She is like us.

I stay close to her, but I know I am not the one she wants.

Dune's Ancestor Journal, December
i have lost enough people to expect death. i didn't expect mine, but i am pretty sure it has happened. it's confusing.
the world will be better when i am gone. i am the result of so

much trauma and pain. i have nothing left in me untouched. my life ended up kinda shitty, i am not special.

and yes, i wanted to kill my husband before he died. doesn't everyone? he never shut up. for decades, he talked almost continuously, whatever he was thinking. as if it were interesting to me. no questions, just pauses where i could grunt in the affirmative.

Sometimes Dune was well into a transmission before she understood it was someone other than Kama, talking story.

he never touched my breasts. he rolled me over and pressed himself into me with his finger and thumb, sometimes yanking me to the edge of the bed first. this was how i got pregnant with my children, can you imagine?

sometimes i still feel the confusion of those years with him. i feel his absence, does that mean i miss him? but that would mean i miss the brute force of him, i miss the bruising grip. he had me under such total control. it's embarrassing, but i felt my purpose in that. the way i feel now, all untethered and uncentered, no one to push against . . . even when i was alive i never felt this wild. am i going to be like this for eternity?

if i had to do it over again, i would either leave him or kill him. i would choose myself somehow.

Marta

Marta sat in her car, looking at the expanse of vines and leaves before her. The weather was dancing with cold-cold and she wouldn't be able to camp out of her vehicle indefinitely. Some childlike part of her brain kept suggesting she climb over the wall, even though she could clearly see that it went up to the clouds, the gold and burnt orange dancing through the vapor. To her left and right, the wall stretched farther than her naked eye could see.

It reminded Marta of the time Kama drove them over to the ruined Packard Plant and talked about the impermanence of capitalist structures and how everything, even a massive car factory, would be swallowed back up by the earth. This scale felt that big, but vertical, reaching into the sky.

Marta wondered if Dune had thought of Kama and the Packard Plant, if the wall looked infinite from the inside too. Marta wondered if Kama would be into the wilderness that had swallowed Detroit. She figured her almost-mother-in-law would appreciate the disruption of it. The seasonal wall had cut off the Ambassador Bridge, one of the busiest points of transit for goods between the US and Canada. It had shut down Detroit Wayne County airport, a huge Delta hub. And so far, it was keeping her out of the only place she wanted to be. She felt put out; of all these people, the wall should recognize her, let her in.

Release

For a few weeks, Berta awaited an invitation from Dune that never came. One day she risked knocking on Dune's door. The Dune who opened up several minutes and rounds of knocking later was pale, like life had been sucked out of her at the wrists. Dune tried to pull off a smile, but her face couldn't do it, so she just turned around and left the door open for Berta to enter. They walked through the sunny open living room to the bedroom, where the curtains were drawn, the ghosts of spliffs past caught in the air. Dune collapsed into the bed and pulled the covers to her chin.

Berta moved quietly around the bed, gathering plates and mugs and taking them to the kitchen sink. She pulled a cedar bundle from her bag and burned it, circling the house and blowing the cleansing smoke into the corners. She hung up Dune's clothes and gathered her laundry into the bin. Dune wept on and off as Berta cleared the container around her, grateful and tired and bottomless.

When the space was somewhat clearer, Berta peeked through the curtains. "The windows don't open in this place? No wonder you're struggling."

Her voice was low, almost to herself. She lit the cedar again and held it over Dune's head, washing it down her grieving body, blowing the smoke as if she was starting a fire. Dune felt the faint tingling presence of energy in her body responding to Berta. Berta left for a minute and came back with a different bundle, one Dune didn't recognize, something dried and long. She lit the cedar a third time and used the mystery bundle to direct the smoke all around Dune, gently hitting Dune with whispering leaves. After an immeasurable while, Dune began to moan. Berta quietly encouraged this, humming, whispering, "yes, yes let that out. Ooooh," smoking clear the spirit around her. Dune's moans became wails, the wails became breath, the breath became an earthquake. Only then did Berta get still and become part of the container. When Dune finally stopped shaking, she fell into deep sleep almost instantly. The day had become night as Berta worked. Now she lit the cedar once more and used it to invite the released spirits and energies to walk with her out of the room, out of the space, and eventually, out of the building. She blew them towards the river, knowing that with spirit you could only ever suggest a direction.

Caught Up

Dune's Ancestor Journal, December
i promise i still grieve you
even though there's no time
and it don't show on my face
there's just so much to do
another apocalypse every few minutes
another death
another one like yours which hurts in a specific way
another one different than yours
en masse, and all alone

Jizo

Dawud had gathered and dragged Dune to the dining room. He was being as tender with her as he knew how. They grieved in such different ways. Dune wanted to crawl under her bed and be alone. Dawud needed to be vibrant and in motion. She would get through this meal, he would not say anything about her sullen countenance, they would live another moment. They were sitting at a table near the door with Mama Tazina, who was staying quiet with them.

"Look," Dawud had no subtle cells in his body, pointing past the bar to a table on the far wall. "Jizo has a friend." Sure enough, Jizo was sitting with someone, a pale brown girl with long straight hair. They were signing rapidly, deep in what appeared to be an engaging conversation. The girl laughed a lot and Jizo looked pleased to be amusing her.

Dawud stood up. Dune caught his hand, "Where are you going?"

"To embarrass my boy. Part of the process." Dawud wiggled his eyebrows, mischievous. Mama Tazina and Dune both made sounds of warning, but he was on his way. Mama Tazina asked how Dune was. Dune was trying to find the kindest way to say awful when Dawud came back to their table so quickly, with such a contrite look on his face, that Dune almost felt bad for him.

"Her name is Hind, she's from Dearborn, and her Dad is one of the chefs. Right now they're in the middle of an important conversation." He sat back down, rolling his eyes. Dune smiled at him with soft eyes, her first real smile since Captain's death. Then she started laughing low in her throat.

"You're not cool anymore," she managed to get out around her laughter. Something about this made her laugh harder and soon they were all laughing, at aging, and youth, and boundaries, and changing, and Dawud's protective pout.

Dune realized she was ready for Dawud to come home.

Dog

The people are going through the change, same as the trees. The trees change, everything gets lighter and lighter until nothing can hold onto anything else and all the leaves fall down. I like to dive into the leaves when they are gathered into piles, but this year no one is gathering them, so I am just rolling around on them, wishing all my people were a bit closer to the ground.

Jizo

A few nights after the dining room sighting, Jizo came to bring Dune dinner. Acorn squash roasted in slices, crispy potatoes, crunchy kale in a lemon vinaigrette, and turmeric brownies. He presented the plate with some flair and signed, "Can we talk?"

"Of course," Dune pulled him into a hug and then held his hand as they walked to the window seat, where there was still some pink light pouring through the wall. Dune missed watching the sun kiss the river on the horizon. Once they were seated, Dune looked Jizo over deeply. His eyes were the same; curious, wide, soft. His hair was growing in, all to one side, thick and shiny.

"Miss you."

"I miss you too, kid. Were you on a date the other day?"

Jizo tried to bite down a smile and a giggle. "Yes, Hind. She's very cool."

Dune's hands begged for more.

"She is so smart. She can make herself unseeable, like me. Not invisible; she just won't register your attention unless she wants to. I never met anyone else who can do that. She really enjoys life. She is so sweet with her family, they're really protective of each other, too. She is helping me remember things."

"What kind of things?"

"Like, before Captain. I have been alive for a long time."

Dune wanted to know everything. "What has she helped you remember?"

"I've been a lot of people's child. I can't remember who was first, but I remember a lot of people, when their hearts broke, I could feel them, as if they were calling to me. Mostly older, but not always. Just lonely, needing someone to care for so they could remember to care for themselves."

Nodding, Dune felt fast tears spill down her cheeks. "Captain wasn't your first assignment."

Jizo lit up. "Exactly. Assignments. I don't remember all of them, but I have some memories. Hind's family was forced out of Palestine when she was six, and they ended up in Dearborn. Now she's trying to remember what life was like, before. Even the hard parts, anything that happened, we already survived. So, we're helping each other."

"That's beautiful, Jizo."

"How are you, Dune?" She realized he was looking at her just as intently as she was looking at him.

"I'm ok, kid. I think losing Captain was kind of a last straw for me." Jizo tilted his head in question and she felt the familiar sweet feeling of speaking to an alien. "It's about the idea of hay straw being very light, but if you pile up enough pieces, they can break your back." He nodded, like he mostly got it. "So I just needed to fall apart for a while."

"Are you really ok now?"

"I think so. I'm coming back into myself. Or at least trying to understand who I am now, and where."

"I don't know who I am now either. I think that's part of why I'm trying to remember, like if there was someone I was before

I started helping people. And if it's ok to be someone else for a while."

"Oh, yeah. I mean, I don't know how the world works anymore," Dune laughed. "But you deserve to feel . . . yourself."

"You too."

Dune felt a flutter of sadness for Captain. She decided to risk a nostalgic invitation. "Uno?"

"I'll grab the deck," Jizo was already in motion.

Dune's Ancestor Journal, December
she's going to eat herself to death
   but why?
she can feel us.
   she can feel us—
   is it too much for her?
no its just . . .
she is eating for thousands

Dawud

Dune was too hurt to look Dawud in the eye.

"It's not what you think, baby."

For the third night in a row, Dawud lay on his back, close to her, with no erection. They hadn't fucked since he came back from his weeks in the Lafayette apartment. She had thanked him for the space and cried with him in their shared grief. Now she wanted him, wanted a messy reconnection. Dune pulled the sheet slowly up her body, not wanting her embarrassment to show, but unable to bear the weight of his eyes on her nakedness.

Since moving into Murmur City, Dawud had gotten a bit soft around the middle. In that same time, Dune had gained just over thirty pounds, transforming every inch of her body. She wasn't hungry, but she couldn't stop eating.

Now, every soft part of her felt like it was about to bruise. Dawud was searching for a way to reject her fat body, she was sure of it. He kept talking. "It's what you know, not what you think. You *know* I love you in any physical form, including extraterrestrial."

Dune was tensed as if for a blow. "Not helpful." He was going to tell her he loved her but he no longer desired her, she wasn't the slender boyish body that could double as masculine—she hadn't quite figured out how to express her boihood in this curved nudity.

"I love you. I'm just worried about the throwing up."

Dune froze. Dune's guides and ghosts froze. Even Dog sat at attention.

Dune *never* threw up when anyone was around. And never on purpose.

"Baby? You ok?" Dawud was touching her now. "I'm sorry . . . I know you don't want me to know."

Dune felt every cell in her body try to get smaller. She felt like he was speaking of something *she* barely knew. *How* did he know? It had to be something horrible. She was able to eke out, "How?"

"Your voice changes. It's all scratchy and smokey after. It's beautiful, but I'm pretty sure it's from throwing up. I noticed when Cap was still here, but couldn't figure out how to bring it up. My only other hypothesis is smoking, but joints never used to do that to your voice, and you don't smell like nicotine." Dawud was speaking to her as if explaining a case study to a comrade.

He let her be quiet for a while. His leg was slung over her thigh and she felt it holding her in place somehow, as if she were unexpectedly a fragile wild creature about to dart away.

She didn't know what to say. It was a subject she had never once in her life considered talking about. She couldn't imagine a more uncomfortable silence. She wanted to do more than leave, she wanted to fold into a quantum realm where no one would even remember she existed.

"Is it because of me?" His voice was nearly a whisper.

"Oh, no." She spoke just as softly. "I don't know what it is, baby. I just . . . sometimes when I'm alone I feel this restlessness. Sometimes it feels like nothing is real."

He reached a hand out, touching her hair, her ear, her jaw.

"Or more like I don't want anything to be real. I don't want to feel anything. I'm not trying to throw up, I just fog out and eat too much."

He bit his upper lip into his mouth; she wondered what he needed to say. He wrapped both arms around Dune and crushed her into his chest. After a little time passed, she realized the combination of stillness, breath, and small shocking hitches in his body was a new way of crying. They lay there, her watching them both from far away inside herself, him stealth crying, her learning he could do it so quietly, him holding her like a lost child, her realizing she *was* dangerously lost, even held.

Slowly the energy in their embrace shifted from comfort to presence—they hadn't held each other in so long. They took turns squeezing each other tighter, a pulsing pressure. Eventually, with gratitude, she felt him get hard against her thigh and she flattened her hand against his belly, slipping, fingers first, under his sweats. Escape.

"Dune," he was so concerned with what was right. Right or not, she needed him inside of her, immediately. She answered with a soft rhythmic grip through her hand. She answered by turning onto her belly and pulling her drawers down. She answered with a slippery welcome and a quick mess. She answered by laughing uncontrollably with him when he came deep inside her, because how incredible was this kind of pleasure despite that kind of pain?

Service

Since Captain's death, Dune and the family had been slowly integrating back into the dining room schedule. Dune had signed up for kitchen shifts, cause working was easier than sitting trapped at a table where people could approach her with condolences. By some small miracle, Rio was on tonight, and they'd both been assigned to dish duty. They danced around each other, proximity its own foreplay, as always.

"Hey, you," Rio said, finally, dimples caving around their full lips.

"I miss you," Dune blurted back, somewhere between embarrassed and proud to be saying the truth.

"Ditto. I've been meaning to come by. I am so, so sorry about Captain."

Dune let the condolences move through her to the places where Captain's absence was an open wound. She smiled her thank you back to Rio. "He was ready."

"Ready to be back with Delilah, huh?" Rio's smile was big enough that Captain could be there with them, alive and dead.

"You know it. He literally said he was going to see her and closed his eyes." They laughed at this until the laughter caught on other things, like their longing for each other, their shared question about whether they were meant to be together, a Captain and Delilah love. The space between them filled with Sahari's fear and their own sweetness. "I miss him so much."

"How's Jizo taking it?"

"He seems to be ok now—he disappeared for a few days and . . . well, you've seen him."

"Yeah, neat trick. Wait, like literally disappeared?"

"No just went somewhere else, we still don't know where he went. I could feel that he was ok?" Dune hadn't shared this with anyone other than Dawud.

"Feel? Whatchu mean?" Rio gave Dune that look she loved, like she was a specimen they had found.

"Everyone I know, I can feel them in here. Like roughly where they are and that they're . . . ok, breathing, alive." Dune closed her eyes briefly and she could feel that Dawud was off to her left, and at ease. He was probably in their place; she couldn't pinpoint where exactly. But direction and presence were clear. "Even you. I can feel you."

Rio looked uncomfortable. Dune clarified, "No details. It's not like seeing . . . just feeling like, the connection." They didn't pick up the rope, both focused on scrubbing and drying the last of a stack of plates. When Rio went down the hall for the next load of dishes, Dune followed, extraneous. As they walked, Rio leaned close. "You know, there's this place in here, maybe you've heard of it? The Cave?" Rio was speaking only for Dune's ears now.

"I've heard rumors. People who think H-8 is contracted through eye contact?" Dune's face showed a gentle doubt.

Rio nodded. "Something like that. I know, it sounds wild. But who knows?"

Dune twisted her lips to keep quiet. She knew. No one had been looking at her mother when the virus came. And her mother had seen no one else after it arrived. Dr. Rogers had confirmed the uselessness of masks long before Dune knew Murmur City existed, saying it would reduce their instances of cold and flu, but do nothing to deter this virus, which was passed through major water sources. Dune felt befuddled by these Cave dwellers—life with the virus was already so hard, why add layers of misinformation and struggle that weren't necessary?

"I think they have some people there with that magic, feeling people. And they have these rituals, like grief rituals. It's pretty private, but I'm sure Kat would like to meet you."

"Kat?" Dune continuously thought that she had seen and met everyone left in Detroit, only to find a new tributary of people, thriving.

"He's an old friend. You'll recognize him, he eats here sometimes. But I guess he's become kind of a pastor in there? He doesn't blindfold."

Dune was listening to Rio, trying to stay in the real world where they were just friends. But part of her was distracted by memory and fantasy and communion and need. She met Rio's eyes, reckless. "Will you take me there sometime?"

Rio understood all the layers in the question. They were almost at the cafeteria when Rio slipped into a pantry. Dune followed, habit. Rio turned around, suddenly closer to Dune than they had come in months. They fingered a frizzed strand of Dune's fro. "I want to be there for you."

Dune's grief barreled through the opening, catching them both off guard as a guttural wail escaped her throat. Dune bucked forward, fell against the wall beside her and sat down hard on the floor, letting the tears come. She was weeping, caught up in the unmoored feeling of having no one before her in the arc of time. She was crying for Dawud knowing her shame, and Rio's ridiculous boundaries, and Jizo growing up, and feeling alone amongst her people. Rio cupped their apron into their hands and covered Dune's face with it, squatting down and pressing against Dune's eyes. Dune cried so hard she couldn't breathe, couldn't control the grimace of grief contorting her face.

Afterwards she blew air slowly between her lips, trying to catch herself, center herself. As soon as the tears subsided, Rio dropped the apron and squatted in front of Dune. "Good job." Honey, love, baby, darling. No endearment was on the other side of the line. "Good job letting that out. Let me know when you're ready to visit the Cave. It will help."

Rio's eyes were massive, attentive, trying to offer all the comfort of touch. It wasn't until Rio stepped back through the door, leaving Dune a moment to gather herself, that she realized Rio had managed to comfort her without actually feeling her skin.

This opened a new wave of grief. Dead or alive, her beloveds were untouchable.

Sahari

Later that night, Rio and Sahari entered their apartment. This was supposed to be a movie night for them, but Sahari had been quiet all the way home and Rio was thinking of Dune's big grief.

"Did you fuck her?"

Rio looked up from their contemplation, shocked. Sahari was standing in front of the closed door, arms crossed. No escape. "What?"

Sahari started speaking, too fast. "I didn't think I would see it. I thought it would definitely happen, but far from me. I definitely didn't think you'd do it while I was sitting in the dining room. Do you hate me? Or did you forget I was there?"

Rio was still off balance, trying to piece together what Sahari was accusing them of.

"When you came out of the pantry you didn't look my way, just went back to the kitchen and, eventually, back to your post. There was something on your apron. Was it... What was it? Cause when Dune walked out she looked undone. Did you fuck her?"

"No." Rio was furious. Dune was in pain and they had shown up to help their friend. They hadn't touched her. And this happened, regardless.

Sahari wasn't registering Rio's emotions, now pacing in front of the door spilling more of her paranoid thinking. "Did you reject her? Did y'all fight? Why did you sneak away? Right in my face?"

Rio looked at Sahari, a woman they had tried loving from so many angles. They thought of Dune, weeping on the floor of a pantry closet and how it had felt to not be able to hold her. Rio thought of the sure thing of Sahari, how they could have 100 percent of Sahari anytime they wanted. But what Sahari wanted was too much somehow, it felt like more than 100 percent. Rio and Sahari could not satisfy each other. Sahari wanted a world where Rio's heart could never love anyone else, and Rio wanted to openly love Dune. It didn't matter how big or small their world was, this impasse was true.

Rio reached out and grabbed Sahari's hand, pulling her to stillness, to face them. Sahari's eyes were flooded with terror. Rio knew that the terror had nothing to do with them and they couldn't clear it. "Sahari. I didn't sneak anywhere. Dune is grieving for Captain and needed to cry for a moment. I held space for that. I needed to show up for my friend. I let her wipe her face on my apron." Rio saw Sahari gearing up for an interrogation. "And this isn't working for me, Sahari. I love you so much, but I can't not be myself. My sacrifice isn't enough for you."

Sahari reared back, "Oh, your sacrifice? *Your* sacrifice?"

"Yes. When we got together, we agreed to a non-monogamous relationship. To avoid this moment right here. And we were *good*. But here we are. You are having a monogamous reaction to me comforting my friend . . ."

"Don't talk to me like I'm crazy. Dune is not your friend."

Rio felt caught. There *had* been an energy when they'd stepped into that room. Any room.

"Right now she is my friend. That is all I have offered her, for months, on your behalf. But you're right. It isn't my truth. And you being mad about that isn't going to change my truth. And me following your rules isn't going to change your truth."

Sahari was so angry, but Rio stayed soft. Sahari's big eyes showed that the path of acceptance ahead was going to be a long one; she wanted a fight that Rio couldn't meet her in. Rio pulled her in for a tense hug, feeling relieved and sad and so tired.

Searching

Mama

Dune caught herself throwing up a week later.

It was never on purpose. She just ate more than her body could hold and her body reacted.

It was never on purpose. She just got high and couldn't tell when she was full.

It was never on purpose. She wasn't even hungry, just restless and wanting to be absent.

It was never on purpose. She just kept filling her plate up with the things that were hardest to control, and bringing extra food back to her room, to eat in private.

It was never on purpose. She just felt the need for a snack every time she was alone.

Before Dawud had mentioned it to her, she'd been able to easily excuse the behavior as occasional, random.

The first time she threw up after Dawud shone his light on her, though, she noticed. She noticed it had been a week because she had thrown up earlier on the night he spoke up, and the sex they'd had that night was the last time he'd been inside her. He was trying not to act differently. For a while it had felt like there was a field of landmines between them; now she knew she was the explosive. She didn't know how to let him be close to this thing happening in her body.

She threw up, acidic and messy. Then she cleared her throat, blew her nose, rinsed her mouth with water and mouthwash, and changed clothes to make sure no smell came with her. She needed to go outside. The service elevator went down to the basement level; she let herself out with a code. The security team would know she had left, but this way she didn't have to run into anyone and fake a conversation.

She took a half-sized electric car off its charger and drove towards the Corridor. She needed to visit her mother. She smoked a joint out the window as she drove, the hydroponic weed nice and strong. As she parked the car near her tree house, the high made her feel clear and present. There was no one in sight, so Dune propped open the car door and sat there, reaching to check on her people. Dawud, check—she could even feel waves of sadness from him. Jizo, check. Rio, check, with some distress. She could feel each person she thought of. So, she thought of Kama.

Kama was here, but there was no direction. Or, she was in every direction. Dune closed her eyes, trying to understand. Kama's presence was as strong as all of her loved ones, but she could have been the air itself. Kama was everywhere. Dune thought of the wall, trying to see—was Kama also everywhere beyond the wall? Dune could sense very clearly that the wall was there, but she couldn't tell if Kama was beyond it. But there was . . . there was someone. Not Kama, not an everywhere spirit, but someone as distinct as those inside the wall. There was someone she loved, outside the wall, close.

Dawud

Dawud sat alone in his studio. It had been a while since he felt the muse, the download of flagrant spirit that led to *Circus* material. He was tumbling with something now, but it felt different than usual. He hit record.

"Maybe we are not redeemable. Maybe, at least, I am not redeemable. Irredeemable Me? Did you ever consider that? That the great *I am* inside your head, inside your heart, is the craziest part, the hungriest part, and maybe has had enough chances? Maybe we're not supposed to be here. Maybe I can't sleep because part of me knows that we aren't supposed to be here. We don't worship the goddess, the dust, the holy, the miraculous, the deep. We are the shittiest fucking species. That's all my theses combined into one existential dread. People telling me to smile through it, to find the sweet spots that remain under the pain ... All I can think is: you've never carried a body, a body that yearned to bear its own weight. But ghosts don't get the privilege of weight. They have to watch others heft it. They have to watch others curse it and conform, bury or burn it, carry storms worth of tears, collapse their breath into shallows, turn in toward the sunken realm, find all of their love and bring it into the light. When the spirit leaves the body, what's left behind is impossibly heavy. The living carry more than the dead—grief weighs more.

"And maybe, maybe I have generated too much grief to carry. Or maybe I have done things no one can recover from. Maybe I am just not one of god's chosen—all of this first world melancholy, why have so much and suffer so deeply for it? What if we were all supposed to die and that was the story? If we were just in the big number for this place, like the tsunami here and the earthquake there and the avalanche and the plague. The plague here. What if we were just part of the plague and we weren't supposed to live and the fact that we did does not make us miraculous, but makes us lost? Lost souls struggling to make a tiny life inside a tiny circle of ambitious vines? Like, what if that is the 'what'? If the meaning of my life is that I overstayed my fucking welcome and now I can't get out?"

Dawud set down the microphone. He laid his forehead down against the table for a moment, his thoughts pulling him under.

He had heard Dune in the shower, crying. He knew with no questions that she was crying because of him. Maybe not because of him, but because he was the buffer between her and her overwhelming grief, for Captain and the city and probably her privacy around this binging, this coping. And her family, always. As completely shitty as this plague had been, it had been years since Dawud's sister had been a part of his life. He'd lost loved ones, but most of his grief predated this calamity, which was likely why he had run towards it. Dune had lost her world and every major character in it. He was still new, and they were almost strangers sometimes, still. And he knew that in her shoes, he probably would have hung himself in that basement. She had dragged her dead into her yard, she had tracked her dead for their patterns. Now she walked the world without them, with just the echo of their weight amassing over her muscles. And she continued. She had foraged, she had learned to make food last, she had found him. And she had the added grief of discovering magic, but too late to save her people.

Now when he held her, he could feel the difference between them in the gravity of how they held what they held. He wanted to share the weight, but she wouldn't give anything up.

He erased the recording.

Dune's Ancestor Journal, December

one of my worst traits when i was alive was searching the faces of people i was around for directions across my own emotional terrain. i felt certain that i should be able to see what they were feeling, and be shaped by it, even though i would never let them see what was under my surface. i had to be very intentional, to climb a mountain inside for every moment of authenticity in the flesh. it's just not how i was raised. it was looked down upon, it was judged harshly, it was considered weak, etc. it just wasn't done.

but then i started to be so hungry for it—when i felt like weeping inside, i wanted to see another cry. when i felt an instance of belonging, i would see that ease on the face of another. as i got older, i learned to make my emotional state louder, more visible. not exaggerated, not false, not a performance. just really bright and obvious. and ok! i wanted it to be ok to feel so much.

you know, even when we are in a body, part of us stays ancestral, or spirit. it's the connective part of us, that's the most consistent self. the furthest we are from connection is when we are so briefly in bodies. but that individual consciousness is a hell of a drug, that sense of aloneness that can go behind walls and fill with solitude.

god told me that so far the experiment of humanity has failed, but she's learning a lot.

Brewing

Dune and Dawud were both weeks deep in their inner battles.

He was becoming more critical, more agitated.

He shaved his head.

He plucked at his beard.

Dune was in a battle with her body each day, saying she was going to do something healthy—eat different, go to the gym, go for a walk. And some days she did, but most days she didn't. She binged. The black hole was gnawing inside her. She was the weight she was lifting.

Dawud's full body ease, which had made it possible for Dune to land into life with him, had tightened into a constant tapping—of his foot on the floor, his fingers against his thighs, his eyes against the boundary that protected her and contained him.

Dune couldn't tell if she was losing herself or losing him. She got slower, staying in bed or on the couch when she wasn't actively going through the motions of maroon life. Her magic tracking project remained theoretical, a commitment from before this depressive dive, a blinking cursor in a blank document.

They were grieving beside each other, neither one knowing how to get to the same side of whatever was currently growing between them.

She felt abandoned. She wanted to be held, touched . . . she wanted Dawud to understand how much it took from her, communicating to the city itself, praying into dirt, generating safety. To understand and to be her comfort, to make her laugh and feel normal and human and small.

Dawud felt claustrophobic, missing Captain and feeling like there was no place big enough for him to have feelings while

Dune had hers. The wall began to look different to him, like a trap more than a safety.

Dune's Ancestor Journal, December
a room of one's own is less helpful these days than some time of one's own.

cultivate listening in the quiet. you need time to make meaning of a life. otherwise, you are just being used by the impulse of procreation. time is what makes a life into a purpose, into a path.

Choices

Dune was watching Dawud pack a bag. He wasn't packing everything, just a duffle to take to the other apartment, but watching him still produced a pulling in her that felt closer to grief than anything else. He caught her looking at him and crooked a half smile.

"Why so glum?"

She hated when he played emotionally dumb. Where they used to orbit each other there was now a constant retrograde.

"I just thought you were here tonight."

"I'm not *not* staying . . . but . . . well so did I, Dune. Like your book says, 'god is change.'" Dawud pointed to the worn Griot collection of Octavia Butler's *Parables* on Dune's bedside table.

"But when did you begin to change?"

Dawud looked away from her in several directions, as if hearing sounds beyond her range.

"Honestly?"

Dune nodded, steadying herself with a breath. She was a tree, deeply rooted. She was a quivering leaf. He sat down near her, facing her.

"Since Captain died, I've been feeling trapped. Not with you, but just like, in Detroit. That wall all around us, in every direction. We're prisoners, in a way. I mean . . ." He scratched his chin as if it needed to come off. "Can we leave, Dune? This wild and gorgeous city? Can we leave if we want to?"

Dune felt shocked, again. She had expected something else about her body. In a way a question about the wall was a question about an extended aspect of herself, but this was so unexpected. She knew there were some rumblings in Murmur City, questions that had made it as far as the edges of council meetings. But she didn't know that Dawud had doubts about the wall, about the protection it offered.

"It isn't *my* city, babe. The city is it's own . . . It's own . . ." She shook her head and hands a bit, chaotic, trying to indicate a word that didn't yet exist. "The wall is protection. For us. It's to keep us safe. To keep the city safe."

Dawud was looking at her with such tenderness, she couldn't help but smile. She needed him to understand.

"What if what feels safe to you feels like prison to me?"

She chewed her inner lip for a moment, looking perplexed.

"Dawud. My parents had a perfect love. Weird as shit but they had it, they knew it early and they built a life together. And for fifteen years they got to love each other, sometimes feeling trapped, sometimes feeling free, rarely at the same time. But they planned on forever; they knew they wanted to figure it out together. They only got fifteen years. It doesn't matter," Dune's voice caught here. "It doesn't matter what we plan. What we want. We get what we get. It just matters that we love each other. We all die, but first we love everyone, everything we can. As much as we can, as long as we get to. I know one day we might have to leave Detroit. Maybe it's already too small to hold you, I hear you. But I need you to hear me—it was created from love. Not control, not even fear. From the love of my parents for Detroit, for me. From our love. From Captain and Jizo, from all the people who died here. So I will never see it as a prison, to me it's how they hold me . . ." Dune's jaw was tight, trying to make the words hold the feelings.

Dawud said nothing, just moved close to her and pulled her onto his chest. She wept, quietly, for Kama, for Brendan, for Mama Vivian, for Elouise. She wept for everyone who was gone and still holding her. She saw their faces, which would never get any older, which were already becoming essential elements—Kama's eyes when she smiled, Elouise's head thrown back in outrageous laughter, her father's hands on his hips, Mama Vivian's face when she was listening to someone she was about to teach a thing or two. Dune keened into his chest, her gratitude for these memories, her bitterness to not get any more. He held it.

And Dune could still feel the wall, now, right here in the room, weaving its untamed barrier between them.

She finally asked, nose stuffed, "Why do you need to go out there?"

Dawud's eyes were so soft. "You keep saying this is for our safety, but I didn't come to Detroit to be safe. And that's not your job. We each have to keep ourselves alive. You met me out there, being a warrior in the wild." He was half joking, but she could also feel that subterranean creatureself, the part of him that always felt like a stranger to her, rumbling in his words. "Shit, I met you out there."

Dune shook her hands out of Dawud's and took his face in her palms. She could feel tantrums in her throat and was determined to keep them there, to root in logic and not emotion.

"That's not what I mean. There's wilderness here, there's a world to make here. This wall is to keep us safe, so we can finally relax and not be on guard all the time, so we can tend to this place. Why isn't that enough for you?"

"It might be. It might be so stupid of me to feel this way." Dawud looked wounded, confused. Cupping her hands, he first pressed them harder against his cheeks, then pulled them back down into the space between them. "But I need to have the option to go. I need to know I can choose. I think a lot of us do. If we can choose, if I can choose, I'll probably stay here and enjoy the safety. But if I can't choose?" He glanced out the window, "I'm going to war against that fucking wall."

He was chuckling as Dune pulled away inside his touch. Dawud was going to war with her. He wasn't leaving her; he was moving against her. And he was right, in a way—she could feel it as he spoke. The city was part of her, she was part of it. She could feel the wall, in the soles of her feet, up her spine, in her fingertips.

"Dune?" Too slow, he noticed her cooling, hardening.

"Go, babe. Please. We can talk more tomorrow." She was holding tight. He searched her face once more and found no opening. She waited for the click of the closing door before she let the tears reach her cheeks. She wasn't going to let her enemy see her weep.

Felt Sense

The knocking at the door was panicked. Dawud wouldn't knock.

Dune wondered who it could be as she moved forward, pulling on a sleep shirt. Was it Jizo? Or Mama Rue? Berta?

But when she opened the door it was Rio. And they looked wrecked.

"Sahari's . . . gone?"

"Do you want to come in?"

Rio paced back and forth in front of the door. "I can't. We fought yesterday and she hasn't come home. Today I came back and a lot of her stuff was just gone. I don't know where she could be."

Dune stepped into the hallway and pulled the door behind her, keeping her hands at her back. Rio was frantic and foggy, walkie talkie in hand. Dune had a million questions, but looking at Rio's face she could tell it wouldn't help to interrogate the fear.

"How can I help?"

Rio paused their pacing. They stepped close to Dune.

"Is she still alive? Can you feel her?"

Dune didn't hesitate. She looked around and saw the ancestors in the way the hall lights landed on the wall, praying in the rug. She closed her eyes, fortified, and reached out into the city in the way that was mysterious to her, but clear. Part of her mind wished Dawud could see her, using the force. Almost immediately, she could feel that Sahari was alive, and relatively close. "I can't tell exactly where she is, but she is alive, and not far."

Rio exhaled with an intensity that bordered on collapse, already rushing down the hall. "Thanks. Thank you. I'll . . . I'll let you know when I find her."

Dune slipped back into her apartment. She closed her eyes and reached for Jizo. He was a bright energy. She reached for Dawud. He was alive. She reached for Kama—she was alive, but in a way that was so different from the others. Dune pulled each of them to clarity until she could tell the difference. Sahari and Dawud were alive and pulsing like campfires. She had the sense that if she focused her skills somehow, she could find them. Jizo was a bright steady light. No pulse, but vibrant. Kama was not bright, not pulsing. She was altar candlelight. And her presence was impossibly clear.

Dune reached for Sahari again.

She was here, somewhere. She was here.

We Fight

Dune's Ancestor Journal, December

we fight differently when we're in the act of sabotage. we are trying to strike the right balance of being unlovable, but not cruel. shaking a lover loose at the heart. he needed to leave me to survive, but he couldn't choose it. he had to make it inevitable. we had to make it inevitable, overtly incompatible, so the only choice where he could not feel shame, the only option i could survive, was to end it all.

we fight differently when we think it's over. we are looking for proof, instead of looking for poetry. we forget to listen. this is one of the biggest regrets i hear amongst the spirits—we forgot to listen.

Hoka

Hoka walked along the river every day. She had always wanted to live on the water. Now that she did, her routine adjusted to include a walk. She let people walk with her as long as they had no expectations—it wasn't a meeting, it was a walk. She also demanded that whoever walked with her took responsibility for their experience, dressing appropriately for the weather. Discussing the weather felt like dying to Hoka.

Dawud sought Hoka out for a walk, and immediately broke her first rule, which was making it a meeting. He asked if Hoka would help him organize Dune into creating an opening in the wall. Hoka's annoyance flickered under her answer.

"There's no way to know for sure, but odds are high that out there, people are trying to figure out how to hate each other in more and more specific and devastating ways. How to strip everyone of their rights while keeping them consuming and consuming, even if the only product left is terror, or repression, or polarization. In here, we are doing what actually matters—figuring out how to be with this living Earth. And look! How it wants to protect us! We are figuring out how to share what we have, how to be with each other. And you know what, it isn't that hard. But you have to set down that other world and get into this one."

Dawud pondered for a moment, "What if something totally unexpected is happening? How do we know H-8 isn't happening everywhere? How do we protect our people from losing hundreds of thousands of Black lives?"

"Someday I would love to spend some time hearing from you exactly who would qualify as *our* people. But today I have to ask: Do you know of a cure that I don't?" She looked up at him, sharp. "We don't know how to protect anyone outside. Not yet. None of our magic can reverse H-8 once it takes hold." Hoka's wrinkles felt louder as she reminded him of this vulnerability.

"No. But we know it's manmade and we know who it targets. Anything man makes can be stopped, controlled, discontinued, regulated."

"By whom? On what authority? I love the optimism, I do. Theoretically. I just think if any of us walk out of here we are walking into unknown conditions that are likely hostile at best. The men who wanted this city enough to enact genocide are most likely watching every inch of our border through trillion-dollar glasses. Greed is the most dangerous human state. Chances are very high that all you accomplish is compromising all of us, either with whatever opening you create being one they can also traverse, or by being someone outside this wall who knows how we work in here, how secure we are and aren't."

"I'm not telling anyone about us."

"Oh, I don't think you would intentionally cause harm to us, Dawud. But there's a lot of ways to learn what someone knows."

Dawud hadn't considered this. They walked back to Murmur City, both in deep and rambling thought.

Dog
Every day this is a new world. The wall brings new smells, smells of a deeper wildness. I am torn. Each time I am close to the wall I want to go into it. But nothing ever comes back. I have chased squirrels and pheasants into the green and as soon as they cross the leaves it is as if they never existed, no sounds of them shaking through the underbrush, no smell. I just have to keep an eye on my humans.

The Point
Dawud was waiting in the dining room, right near the door. Dune cursed him for knowing she'd have to eat eventually. She

looked caught when she saw him, quickly pretending she hadn't. She gave a small performance of forgetfulness with her face and turned to leave.

He followed her toward the elevator banks.

"Dune, stop. Why are you so mad at me?" They pulled into an alcove—it wasn't private enough, but the energy between them couldn't be quiet another step.

"I'm not mad." She was fuming. "You're the one leaving."

"I'm not leaving. You literally know exactly where I am at all times. And you are currently running away from me. I just want to talk. I want to know what our options are. I want to—"

"Do you have a better plan, D? A better idea? To keep all of us safe? Cause it's not just about you and your wild man tendencies. It's not just what I want. This might be our only chance." Dune said "our," meaning humanity. She felt Kama in her hands as they pierced and sliced the air. Unlike her mother, her voice got quieter and quieter as she got more honest.

"That's not the point, Dune."

She whisper-screamed at him, "Then what is the fucking point, Dawud? Cause those people almost killed everyone in here. And they absolutely will kill us if they can get through! And they will lie about it! You and I are alive to argue about this because there is a wall between us and those who would kill us!"

"You really don't get it, do you, babe?" He was looking at her like he loved her, which enraged Dune.

"No. I really don't." Dune was developing a new wrinkle between her eyebrows. She wished they were behind a million soundproof walls.

"Baby, everyone here? They . . . We didn't ask you to save us." Dawud looked like it hurt him to be the one to say this to her.

Like she should know it. She felt cold. "This wall is brilliant, it is. I'm not being ungrateful, that's not it. But don't act like it's insane to not want to live inside a fucking wall, not knowing anything about the world outside, with just whoever happened to be in here on a random Tuesday in March! For the rest of all time!? Don't act like this was the result of a collective process. Don't act like your wall is the only option for safety."

"Even if it is?" Dune spoke with exasperation. This was the aspect of collective process that had always kept her from fully committing to the groups her parents created and gave their lives to, this sense of having to deny the obvious in the name of consensus.

"Even if it is." Dawud could at least concede to some logic. "If there's no door, it's a prison. Tell the wall we need a door."

"If there's a door, *they* will find it. They *will* come in." Dune looked at Dawud now with her hands splayed open. Could he see her at all, see that the woman he loved was the child of a murdered mother?

"Maybe."

She collapsed a bit. He was so committed to his theoretical freedom in the face of her tangible grief and fear.

Dawud kept talking, "We have no idea what they are seeing or trying out there. We know that they can't seem to get through, and they don't seem able to fly over, but we don't really know what they're up to. We can guard a door, Dune. One door. I'm literally a guardsman, and you used to think that was hot."

He smirked as she sucked her teeth.

"I never thought that was—"

"Dune, don't lie. Anyway, we can protect it. Without a way out, it's like we all belong to you. Are we here to make *you* feel safe in community?"

"What? Me? I was good on my own."

Dawud threw his fists on his hips like a grandpa. "You came and found me. You yelled 'Stella' in the streets. You needed me. We needed Captain. And Jizo. And this place. It's ok to need it, but we all get to determine what happens, we have to."

"You say 'we' like—"

"It's a lot of us, babe."

Babe sounded hard in his mouth now, drained of endearment, used like a specific tool to remind her of how close they'd been.

Dune understood.

Finally, she understood.

He was going to leave her and even in her fear-based ideations, she had never thought that would happen. Even though everyone else had left her. He was willing to leave, he was itching to leave. And, embarrassingly, he'd been talking with others, building this plan of departure with enough people to constitute a "we."

She had outgrown his love when she had changed from being a person to being a city.

Dune softened her face into a mask. She would not show him her chaos, fearing she would come apart at each seam. She could not show anyone. She felt like the earth trembled a bit beneath her.

"Ok. Ok—I'll see what I can do. I'll speak with the council and, if that's the collective will, I will see about a door."

Dawud was so surprised at her pivot that he almost fell. Then his brown eyes softened, as if this made them closer. He moved towards her as he hadn't in weeks. He wrapped his arms around her waist and held her in his way, a bit too tight.

She held him around the shoulders, feeling breathless at the knowledge that he was leaving. He was ecstatic at the chance to leave her. He may have been giggling against her chest. She thought of how many earthquakes the dirt quelled, without notice or gratitude.

She looked over his bald head, through the window, at the city she felt breathing. The door would be cut from her heart.

Spotting

Almost daily, Dune found herself drawn to the Code Midnight Reading Room, even if it was just for a few minutes of quiet. The snow glare made it too bright most of the time, but she could sit quietly, and it was one of the only places in Murmur City that wasn't thick with Dawud imprints and memories.

Sahari had been missing for a month when Dune looked up from her meditation one morning and spotted her, across the room, leaning against the wall. Dune had known that Sahari was alive and still in Murmur City. She couldn't pinpoint her—she barely knew her, and Sahari didn't want to be seen.

Until she did.

Now here she was: bald, gaunt, her big brown fawn eyes directed out the window. Dune felt annoyance, wanting a moment that wasn't about other peoples' dramas and needs. In the next second, she felt embarrassed, stingy. She didn't rush to speak and wasn't even sure if it would work for her to try and bring Sahari home. Maybe it was enough to know she was alive, and somewhere she could be spotted.

Dune closed her eyes, turning inwards to her own thoughts for a while, her own griefs, gathering herself. When she looked up, Sahari was gone from the wall. Dune looked around the space, feeling some doubt about not grabbing her in some kind of citizen's arrest. But there she was, by the door, watching Dune look for her. Their eyes locked and Sahari didn't run. Dune moved towards her, and Sahari didn't run. When Dune reached her, Sahari stretched out a hand to shake. Though they had spoken and shared space, Dune understood the need for this formality—they had never really talked, and they were about to.

"Go for a walk with me?" Sahari asked.

Precarity

A Big Deal

In Sahari's extended absence and Dawud's growing critique, Dune and Rio had been spending more time together, finding each other, under the permissive umbrella of fresh grief. As much as Dune still wanted Rio, but their romance felt mutually paused in this moment so murky with crisis and confusion. Rio called it letting the mud settle. For now, no discussion of their relationship was needed; just being able to talk was so valuable.

The frequency of their time together meant Dune couldn't avoid Rio in the aftermath of seeing Sahari; she had to find a way to tell Rio about Sahari without betraying anyone.

Dune asked Rio to walk the Dequindre Cut with her the day after seeing Sahari. She wanted to comfort her beloved without betraying the woman who lived between them, the one who so righteously feared her. The Dequindre Cut was a reclaimed train track, now flanked by weathered murals; it provided some distance from the towers. And with the chill of winter in the air and the slightest dusting of snow on the ground, they were most likely to get privacy outdoors. Dog ran ahead of them and back, youthful, kicking the snow up and trying to run through it. Dune wondered if Dog had ever experienced the real Detroit winters, the ones when the snow covered the family car and she and Brendon would have a competition to dig it out. Dune felt foggy and unfocused, wondering briefly how the two of them looked—pretty them Rio out for a snow walk with the hermit boi.

Rio was tense and fast next to her, and as soon as Dune noticed, they stopped and blurted out, "Is she dead?"

"What? No!" Dune stumbled trying to answer while looking at Rio. They caught her, then held them both still for a moment before pulling at Dune's arm like a child.

"Why are we out here? I know you know something." Rio's sweet, brown face was pale from winter and pink from the cold. They looked more vulnerable when they tried to be tough. Dune reached a hand over and grabbed theirs, glove to glove.

"I'm sorry, yes, Sahari is why we are out here. She's alive."

"Like you *feel* her or—"

"No, I saw her, yesterday, in the Reading Room. She let me see her. We spoke." Dune felt for her own center, for the ground beneath her feet. It seemed far. "She apologized."

Rio was already quietly crying, waiting.

"She said she was sorry for how she reacted to me, said she's just been really scared to lose you. I apologized to her too, I told her I never meant any disrespect. She said she was giving you room." As Dune spoke, Rio's face was changing rapidly; relief, anger, confusion, laughter, concern, racing across their delicate features.

"Room?" Rio turned and looked at the buildings of Murmur City, the silver rosette of towers.

"Yes. She . . . she didn't give me a message for you. She said y'all would talk when the time was right." Dune was trying to make a small boundary around the talk she'd had with Sahari. It felt private, it felt like one she wouldn't want retold. Sahari had been so shaky, so raw, but she had also extended some trust to Dune for the first time.

Rio turned back to Dune, searching her face and making a decision. "Dune . . . There's a lot I haven't told you about Sahari," Rio frowned, self-conscious. "She struggles more with her mental health than she shows. . . And she can manipulate things, people . . . Her mind is looping. When she's looping, she's not safe, inside herself. So, if y'all talked, if she gave any indication of what she's doing right now, what she thinks she's doing, I need to know."

Dune felt the gut drop of being out of her depth, a guilty child speaking to an adult. She thought about Sahari, about how clear and intense her energy had been, how fragile she'd looked. Had Sahari been using her in some way?

"Ok, she seemed really . . . Her voice was shaky, she looked really thin. She looked like someone in intense grief. I kept trying to ground with her energy and it was like she was knocking me away, even though her words were all . . . conciliatory." Dune remembered Sahari's eyes, constantly moving.

Rio looked frustrated. Dune wished she could just let Rio comb through the memory. "Does it seem like she really understands what's going on right now? She left me with *no* communication. To me that's a sign of a serious mental break. I have never actually witnessed her having one but I know she has had them before."

"Now that we've spoken, I think I can find her." Dune turned to walk and Rio grabbed her arm. Dune saw the panic. She reached for Sahari, and immediately felt her, a weak, dim light. "She's in the Heart Tower . . . Like, in the basement?"

"She's in the Cave?" Rio started to run and then turned to face Dune, jogging backwards, "Dune, did she say anything else?"

"She said I could have you. I said that's not what either of us wanted. Like it's not a competition. She said I was lying, and that I didn't need to lie, that I could have you. She said she was healing and she was getting herself together, and that she was gonna stay at the Cave until she felt ready. She was crying, she said she was really embarrassed." Dune dropped her head, feeling exposed.

Rio landed something, and nodded, turning back to run full speed, yelling over their shoulder, "I gotta go find her!"

Dune nodded. She had made this thing about herself to such a degree that she hadn't understood the danger Sahari was actually in. "Go!"

Rio took off running. Dune walked back to Murmur City, realizing she still had no idea where the Cave was.

When Rio came by late that night, they looked exhausted. By the time they'd reached the Cave, Sahari was in the throes of an overdose. She was alive, but weak and on an IV. Rio wasn't surprised. Relieved, confused, guilty, exhausted, and grateful, yes, but not surprised. "They sent me away. They are taking care of her. Now they know what they need to know."

Dune broke the boundary then, intentionally reaching out and pulling Rio into her arms. When Rio wept, she wept with them, until they fell into deep sleep together on the couch. That quiet embrace was the most honest either of them had been in a year.

Oh, Great Spirit

Dune was sitting in the corner of the Atrium, the huge glass-walled space that opened onto the River Walk and still had cars on display from the last Auto Show. At the cooks' request, they'd started serving breakfast in here with more self-serve options. Today, she'd waited by the grill to order an omelet, needing to be cooked for. She was wearing new ruts in her brain—how to reach Dawud, how to help Mama Rue, how to support Rio, how to map magic, how to be in her bones, how to get more sleep, how to know what to do next.

Bineshii and her sister friend Sharon came strolling over. For a brief instant Dune regretted coming down to breakfast—she could have had oatmeal in the room and been left alone. But their eyes looked bright.

"Come sing with us." Bineshii watched Dune until she began to stand up, then turned and marched off. Dune followed. Bineshii and Sharon were thick in different ways—Bineshii's broad chest rivaled Sharon's soft hips—but they moved quickly. She recognized the walk, over to the gardens where they grew their food and fish in raised beds and tall vats of water, overseen by grow lights and the Grown in Detroit gardening collective. When they walked into the room full of fish, Bineshii set down her purse and jacket, and both women slipped out of their shoes. Dune followed suit.

"Go ahead," Bineshii said to Sharon, whose warm black eyes kept moving between Bineshii's certainty and Dune's soft cluelessness.

Sharon was a mountain of a woman, filling the room even though she couldn't have been taller than five feet. She moved with a smile on her face, seeming to have a joke in mind. She caught Dune's eye.

"These fish are here for sacrifice, here to feed us in an unnatural circumstance. There is no river, no lake, no sea, no place to truly be themselves. They are alive, but in these strange containers that look like none of the waterworlds they have always known."

As Sharon spoke, she started moving slowly amongst the vats, shoulder high white containers each holding a different breed of fish: tilapia, catfish, bass, trout, and salmon. "We set up the initial system with vegetables down the hall and the fish in here, but we were always planning a full aquaponics structure."

Dune let her ignorance show. Sharon smirked just with the edges of her mouth. "Aquaculture is growing these fish. Hydroponics is growing plants without soil. Aquaponics allows the fish and the plants to nourish each other. Two crops growing from one set of resources. Soon, each of these vats will be topped with lettuce and cucumbers, our watery greens. And then we will repurpose the lettuce beds for something else, probably potatoes cause that's all the kids want to eat."

Sharon was proud, Dune realized. "And you ... sing to them?"

Bineshii and Sharon showed matching smiles then. "Every creature is deserving of total freedom. Even though these fish are bred in here, they are connected to all the fish that ever lived. Being alive in such limited conditions can be very stressful for them; some of them start harming themselves or each other, trying to find more room, to get out, get somewhere. We come to sing to them every day, with different people."

"To zone them out?" Dune felt that familiar sadness of delayed responsibility she often felt when Bineshii was teaching her about yet another relationship Dune had neglected because it never occurred to her that it existed. To Bineshii and Sharon and their Anishinaabe kin, everything was related, and every relationship impacted the world.

"To thank them. We know something about being a creature of god in a fraction of dirt. Watching someone claim to own heaven, and deciding where we can keep breathing. We know about finding a way. So we thank them for making this sacrifice in this lifetime, that we may be nourished." Now the women were shifting into the seriousness of their task. Sharon was donning her shawl, Bineshii wrapping up her long hair into a knotted bun at the base of her neck. "I'll teach you the song; I learned it from a traveling Eno River sibling. We will sing it to every vat."

Sharon's way of teaching was just singing the song, over and over. It worked. Soon Dune was singing the song as if her body had always known it, moving slowly with the women through the space. The tilapia looking up at her revealed themselves as holy beings in scaled robes, their constant motion a form of prayer.

Thank you for every breath I take
Thank you for every day you make happen
for me—I know it's a miracle—MIRACLE

Thank you for all the Love I feel
Thank you for showing me you're real
inside my life / I know I'm so blessed
I'm so blessed

Thank you for every heart that breaks
thank you for all the love it takes
to give this life a chance—

I am grateful I am grateful

Mama Rue

"Don't give up. What you're trying to learn is hard and the only teacher is the doing." Mama Rue was tying herbs into bundles to dry. The space smelled like sage, juniper, lavender, and something Dune couldn't quite name yet—lemongrass?

Mama Rue's hands were seasoned in this work; she easily lined the herbs up next to each other so that one end was even and the other was a wild bouquet. Twine woven through and around the herbs about halfway down the bundle. Once she got these together, she would use clothespins to hang them, even side up, around the edges of the indoor herb garden. "Take a break if you need to. Don't give up."

"I haven't given up." Dune's face fell a bit, like her own words had hurt her. "Maybe I have. I keep thinking maybe it doesn't matter, that my mom lived, that my dad lived, that they died. That I will die, that I lived a bit longer, that I experienced things that maybe no other human has. Maybe it doesn't matter. Maybe none of it matters. And if it's that, then why am I over here in fucking shambles."

"And then what."

Dune glared at Mama Rue. "What?"

"If it is true that none of it matters, but you are still in *shambles*," Mama Rue cut her eyes at the drama, "then what?"

"Then why live?" Dune felt a tantrum brewing in her chest. She wanted to be taken seriously, to scare the old woman into taking her seriously. Because that would mean something mattered.

Mama Rue didn't stop her work, but she set her eyes on Dune while her hands kept moving. "Are you asking me cause I'm old? Are you asking me to convince you? What do you want?"

Dune opened her mouth to scream at her elder, then snapped

it shut. They both felt the rage blossom and pass between them. She closed her eyes the way Berta had taught her to. She took a breath into her length, up through the crown of her head and down through the soles of her feet. She took a breath for her width from shoulder to shoulder. She took a breath from back to front. She settled into her root, her pelvic bowl, her center. She opened her eyes and Mama Rue was still, watching her.

"It matters and it doesn't matter, Dune." Mama Rue sounded different, clearer, fully here. "That's the thing. If you choose not to live, it will matter to the people who love you. It will devastate them. Us. Shit. And then everyone will keep living until they too die, and they will feel your absence for the rest of their lives; that will matter. And then everyone who knew your name will die, even if you have a massive impact. If people do know your name and some piece of your story, it will be tied to their projection or interpretation of what you said, what you did, through their modern lens. If you choose to live, you can make everything matter. Even the smallest things, remembering to eat something nourishing before something sweet, drinking enough water, the murmur of a room full of people who feel safe. You know what it's like to lose everything, you already know that. Everything could matter to you at any moment. Your choice."

Mama Rue leaned in then, a silly look on her face. "Stop pulling me into your linear, pedestrian shit. Come help me hang these."

Dune stepped next to Mama Rue and began scooping up herbs to hang. As they worked, quietly, Mama Rue leaned over and kissed Dune on the cheek.

Dawud

Dawud was standing in the doorway of the home that had been theirs. He had knocked, like he didn't have a key, like his stuff wasn't in the closet. He spoke in his usual matter-of-fact tone.

"I need you."

Dune rolled her eyes, turning and walking back into the apartment. "That's the crisis?"

"Yes. For me it is," Dawud followed her, closing the door behind him. She hitched herself up onto the kitchen counter and he stood, arms crossed, facing her. "I think I came here to die, Dune. Not consciously, at the time—but you don't run towards a plague unless some part of you is ready to go, curious about your own death, your own resistance. I came home to see if everyone I loved here was dead. And they were. And I was supposed to carry on after that? With all of them dead, at once? For me, in my heart, it was everything, gone, all at once. I went numb. I acted like my heart was outside the dumpster fire. I diminished my loss. We aren't meant to lose life at this rate; this much grief is just a kind of insanity. But this is what it's going to be like now, for everyone, for so many reasons, all of it unnecessary, all of it disrespectful to the miracle of this life. I came here to grieve myself to death. But I didn't die. And then, there you are. Here you are. A *fucking lesbian*."

Dune squared up her chin at him. "I ruined your life."

"No. You changed my trajectory. You gave me a reason to do shit. You answered the call. You are . . . magic. Humble. Clueless. And weirdly hot. And not . . . annoying. If *anyone* had even the slightest chance of convincing me to imprison myself, it's you."

Dawud moved as if, in his imagination, he was bowing deeply. His voice got quieter. "But no one can convince me to imprison myself, my love. No one, not you. Not even me."

She was smiling, but she was crying. He leaned forward and kissed her face, the tears there softening and salting his lips.

"Ok," Dune said. She thought of what Mama Rue had said, that whatever happened here needed to be her choice. She could choose to let Dawud see her more clearly. "I do love you. I had no expectations with you, I really thought you were a side quest. But now I feel like the chances I will lose you are so high . . . Sometimes I can't breathe when you're out of sight. And I want you to . . . not matter to me. This much. Like I know I'm going to lose you, but when? How?"

He was nodding. "I know. Like I think everyone here feels that though. About everyone we love, or like or whatever. Like, that shit is justified. We lost everything. We have to hold that in one hand even as we try to hold each other. Choice is a part of being alive."

Dune sniffed. "But you thought the wall was genius."

Dawud shrugged. "I thought we were all dying. It felt like a genius way to go. But now we are like some little commune ass shit and it's dope. And now I want to live, I really want to live. But every day the wall feels like it's closing in on me."

"But I don't even know if I *can* do anything about the wall, Dawud. I really don't."

"I know you can, babe. I know it. And I am willing to have sacred spell-casting sex anywhere to help out."

Dune laughed so hard she snorted. Dawud looked pleased with himself.

"Geniuses can be wrong, too. New info can change geniuses' minds."

Dune grabbed his shirt and pulled him in. This embrace had no borders.

Part 3

Winter, Connect Underground

The Cave

Dog
The people under the building know about respect. They cover their eyes, look down when I approach. They don't feel fearful, they just feel like humans who are tired of how the world is. This is how they feel to me; when I curl up against them, I'm a comfort they didn't expect.

Eye Contact
This was Dune's first time in the Cave, the basement level of the innermost channel of the Heart Tower of Murmur City. This is where people who thought the virus might spread through eye contact spent their days. A lot of people who lived in the hotel rooms up above never came down here. The Cave consisted of a lobby, a small ballroom, and a set of windowless offices that had probably been administrative or janitorial. What Dune noticed immediately, in the glass-walled ballroom, was that there was no overhead

light here, just a few plug-in candles in the center of the room, with people sitting on found pillows, or a few rows of office chairs and benches, all in a big slightly chaotic circle. Simple and shadowy.

Rio had originally invited Dune to the Cave because they thought it was time for her to meet Kat. They were finally bringing her, now that they knew Sahari was safe. It was time for Dune to experience this tender core of Murmur City.

On their walk to the Cave, Rio told Dune that many of the people who stayed close to the Cave were people whose primary work was to grieve. They hold the quiet.

Kat didn't have a blindfold on and clocked them at the window. Kat was a wide, Black masculine person in a plaid button down with a fresh fade carved to look like a wave along the left side of his head. Rio said Kat used masculine pronouns, and that was easy for Dune to see. He was holding court now, with a circle of people, some of whom wore blindfolds. He gave a small wave, a tic of the hand really, an upstroke of chin. As they moved closer to the heart of the room, Dune could see that Kat sat behind a cloth altar on the floor, anchored by a bowl of water and stones surrounded by things that could be burned by visitors—sage, cedar, palo santo, beeswax candles. He kept speaking.

"What I'm saying is, in order to truly face all of our grief, we'd have to face that there is a lot of uneven grief; grief for losses that are unnatural. Everything that lives also dies, that's the contract of the sacred cycle. There is enough of everything for everyone, as long as everyone dies. Ain't that something? And that's only as long as there's a cycle that can continue.

"But the uneven grief means that some of us are not facing our mortality, not operating in right relationship to the miracle of Earth life. Extractions are violent, of resources beyond need, or of nonconsensual care. We accumulate without reason. You feel me?" The crowd responded enthusiastically. "And everything is out of balance. We are not meant to hoard across generations; we keep showing them the dust and gems of raided tombs, but they won't listen.

"I promise you this, my wife taught me this when she was dying: you take nothing with you but your love."

There were several affirmative moans and mmhmms amongst the audience. One blindfolded woman, slender and holding tight to her elbows in a threadbare cardigan, lifted a hand up to the sky in praise.

"Yes, I know you know what I mean," Kat continued. "And we don't stop loving. We never stop. Some ancestor whispered into my ear. She said, 'Our love makes the dirt. Our love sways the branches. Our love burns the cedar. Our love pours down on you as we grieve for you.' What you grieve is grieving you! Without a body to weep from, imagine!"

"Preach now pastor," called out a blindfolded Black man, slapping the arm of his chair. Dune noticed that the patterns on the carpet looked like crowds and crowds of afro'd humans, and that the walls in her periphery were clearly massive silhouettes, stoic and attentive—spirit was present and accounted for.

"You see, grief is when you really grown, however old you are when it happens. You don't really understand what life is if you don't grasp its random brevity. And once you do, you have to grapple with whether you'll ever love again. It is incredibly brave to love when you know what grief is. Every time, in every way, because you fall in love knowing that there will be grief in the future and you dig deeper and deeper, knowing that space will be full of grief one day."

The circle was louder as this wisdom moved through all of them. Some people were openly emotional, weeping. Others were quiet, but Dune could recognize the shoulders that carried unnatural grief. It was amazing to just feel that she was not alone in all her loss. She turned to catch Rio's eye, but they were looking the crowd over, probably scanning for Sahari.

Dune knew that everyone in Murmur City, in Maroon Detroit, was a survivor with a long list of griefs. But it was easy to function as if this weren't the case, as if the to-do list, the safety measures, the day's agenda and the things to be mended, the negotiations, the arguments and miscommunications, the next contact from her lover—as if those were the things that made up her life. But in a way grief was what made up her life. The rest was how she moved one step at a time into a future that didn't include her mother, her father, her friends, her home.

"And I can testify that love is worth it—worth the grief. But you got to know the cost, and protecting your heart from that pain has some wisdom in it . . . although then, why bother? Love is the point, far as I can tell. And I'm not going to start lying to you now. Grief doesn't make you a better person. I mean . . . it can. You can face your mortality and realize that so much of what matters is small and intimate, is about kindness. Or you can become bitter, think life is a cruel game. Whatever you make of that loss becomes your worldview.

"I've been holding my grief as praise, like Martin Prechtel taught us. He said 'grief is praise,' praising with tears and your whole body, how incredible and tender and deep the love was that you felt, how shocking the distance between death and life. Grief is *devotion*. You must give yourself over to it fully if you want it to ever pass, to ever be bearable."

Dune was biting her lip harder than was comfortable, the pressure of her teeth creating a dam within her. She didn't want to be seen in her grief, at least not as a first impression. But by the time she noticed her teeth, it was too late. Her face began the small tectonic shift of collapse, and she leaned forward into her hands, crying as quietly as she could. Rio stepped closer, not touching, but comforting, nonetheless.

"And on the other side of the grief, there is this power. This soft, supple power that understands what matters. The only way to reproduce power that is soft is to grieve, because power involves letting go and moving forward. It takes power to lose your loves and keep going. What do you know about power if you've never slipped your fingers into death's mouth and begged him to take you? And he doesn't? He leaves you here. To live your life. And when you die, when you inevitably die, you will only take your *love* with you. I believe this, because I can feel my love even now across time and space. Love is what matters here and everywhere. Oh, oh my darlings . . . Love is the ticket! Love is the password, the code, the key. Everything you truly love becomes the texture of your eternity."

Dune could feel, directly at the heart of her body, her vast love, her mother father love, contained but infinite. She could hear the tears falling all around her. Her love compounded somehow by knowing it was a feeling flowing through everyone here. She felt so clearly that she knew who and what she loved.

She wanted to stay in this cave. This windowless, candlelit cavern. This shadowy place where everyone looked somehow connected. She wanted to sit here and listen to Kat for days.

After the service ended and people had gone over to thank Kat, Rio and Dune approached the pastor. He smiled at them, lopsided and flirtatious.

"Wasn't that some good grief?"

Dune wasn't sure what to say. Rio made introductions to clear some space for the hello. What came to Dune was a fist bump. Kat made a very serious face before placing his fist against hers.

"I hear you're a singer," Kat said, catching Dune off guard.

"Heard what?" The three of them each issued a different kind of laughter.

"You the one goes around with Mama Rue, right? Singing people back to life? Angelic blues medicine?"

Dune felt a wave of stage fright, like Kat was going to ask for a performance. But Kat reached out and put a hand on her arm. "Hey, I'm just making sure that's you so I can say thank you. I have heard from those who have been touched by your voice. Thank you." Kat's touch was a gift—soft, connected, somehow catching Dune's whole spirit. "Sometime, I will have y'all come and sing me back to life. I'm a mess."

Dune laughed, a little melody crossing the back of her mind, "variations on a mess . . ." She focused. "Thank you. I never think of myself as a singer, it only works as medicine."

"Those are the best gifts, where it's just true. Where other people call on the song because they know it can flow through your instrument. One day you will make medicine for the collective."

Dune felt that she was being organized or recruited or softened, but it was so overt that she didn't feel uncomfortable. A pastor is always trying to grow the flock—that is the job.

"Thank you. I always think there is something better to do. But singing is what comes."

"Can you imagine where we would be without Mahalia Jackson catching those phone calls of doubt? Singing back a response, on demand. Drawing on faith?" Kat shook his head. "I cannot and do not want to. But I am really glad you came here. Can I show you around?"

Rio checked that Dune could find her way home from the Cave, then excused themselves, distracted. Kat talked steadily about everything under the sun as he guided Dune through a strange land that already felt like home. Much of the Cave was like any other part of Murmur City, but a lot of doors had been removed, and the halls were as clear as possible. Dune learned that the space was designed to be navigated by the blind, because so many blind and blindfolded Detroiters survived the initial wave of H-8 that a theory of survival developed.

"I figure whatever you were doing, keep doing that," Kat spoke of the choices lightly. "I was looking at the world while everyone died around me and I didn't die, so I don't blindfold cause that's clearly not *my* survival technology. But for the people here, who am I to tell them what to do?"

Dune had so many questions. "Have y'all heard that we now understand H-8 to have spread through the water?"

Kat looked at Dune with a smile that was full of shrug. "This place works. We hear things all the time, but mostly, in here, we are unchanging. Everyone is free to survive in whatever ways work best for them. It's a really small group of people who still blindfold. I have definitely held the hands of some people as they took off their blindfolds and risked death, and lived. The important thing is that people know they can be supported to *be* here."

Dune's Ancestor Journal, January
time doesn't exist here, so we don't know how to tell you most of the things i want to. but we exist and so i will. i remember all my

deaths, but they feel like something of soft importance, sometimes a silly mistake on my part or someone else's. sometimes an inevitable passageway to a next lesson.

once i was hit by a car and we were still very alive, but we couldn't tell anyone and no one could get my body going again so i waited until everyone was ready to let go and i left.

one time we lit a match when the gas had been on and i had the thought, oh fool, before i was dead.

one time i was lynched and we hung there spiritually for such a long time, not in my body. it's so unnatural to die because of someone's desire to kill you or kill a part of you. death is definite, so being rushed along in it, it's the ultimate insult really and you have to contend with it and let your spirit rest and not take it personally. i was so glad our children kept coming back once my body was gone and being with my spirit until we were truly dispersed from that place.

we remember that as clearly as i remember my small child becoming superhuman to drag my body thru the house and burn it in the yard because i had died inside our skin. that was the strangest death we can recall because we were not alive, but we could not get out of the trappings of recent aliveness. my heart was beating like it didn't know what had happened. i was in my body and couldn't hear anything outside of it and there were so many memories in there, in my bones, my tissues—we remembered every bruise and every delight. we mapped out my life in there, visiting and revisiting until my heart mercifully stopped. only then could we sense my child and my home, and notice what was happening.

spirit is all around you, but we cannot invade your privacy, did you know that? if you do not want to be seen we cannot watch you. my child wanted to be seen by me sometimes, and sometimes by her father. even though he and i are part of everything now, we could only see what she showed us. we couldn't even discuss it amongst ourselves, what we witnessed. we could not share the moments. we didn't know she was building an altar until she brought my bones to it.

animals don't discriminate between the living and the dead. they see us all if we choose to be visible. we can ruin a quiet that way, letting a dog know we're around. we only know if it's day or night if a human or place we're visiting is awake or dreaming. we can slip alongside certain states of consciousness when a living mind is sort of afloat, meditating, untethered from any particular focus or purpose.

we are peripheral and we must admit, with love, that it's hard to sustain interest in the constant doing of the living. we are supposed to rest between lives, we think, but the child isn't ready for us to rest, and it just takes one living obsession to hold us close. we do what we can, communicate what we can. that which is mine still serves us in some way. that child is mine. those bones were mine. those altars are mine. that house is mine. we're beginning to understand that there is no magic, but there are spirits everywhere, affecting everything. partnering with the willing in ways that mystify the living.

Lucinda of the Cave

"Lucinda is a seer."

Kat's invitation had been that simple: Dune needed to be *seen*—read, reflected, understood in a different way. And that's what Lucinda did.

So, Dune was back in the Cave. She thought there would be a crowd, given Kat's hype, but when she slipped in there were only three other people in the room, huddled. They spoke quietly, not as if they were trying to communicate in secret, more like the entire space was quiet. Everyone's volume was low, intimate.

Lucinda had a face that looked baked to perfection, age spotted and soft and papery, busy around the mouth, as if she were processing some small cud. The Cave felt very different with her at the center than it had with Kat. Close to Lucinda were a myriad of tools for divination: several tarot decks, a stack of books, three large shells, and all kinds of herbs. Dune wondered if Mama Rue and Lucinda knew each other.

Lucinda looked up, staring Dune directly in the eye. There was so much in the elder's gaze that it took Dune a while to realize no one was speaking. In Lucinda's eyes she saw peace, she saw pain that had left its mark, she saw ghosts—she felt her own ghosts all around her and knew Lucinda could see them as clearly as she saw Dune. Being beheld by this woman's eyes was a new level of being stripped bare.

Lucinda was not directly in front of Dune and then she was. The elder reached forward to tie a strip of dark cloth across Dune's eyes. It smelled of palo santo and campfire and salt. She held Dune's hands at the wrists, the flat pad of fingertip finding Dune's racing pulse. Dune felt an immediate flow of energy through her body, a relaxing, a slowing down and deepening.

It became clear to Dune that there was nothing quiet in this place. With her eyes closed and covered, she could hear every slight motion around her. She could sense the direction, she could hear the breath of the room and the pounding of her own heart.

With her eyes covered, she could feel how full the room was. She could make no distinction between flesh and spirit, and there were so many people in here. She could feel the elemental nature of the crowd, that they were flesh bags of water, that they were fire-breathing dragons and pounding animate dirt and tornadoes on leashes of social norms. The room was more pattern than person—being deprived of sight was almost like being disarmed by a drug; her senses were flooded with data.

Lucinda eventually placed her hands on either side of Dune's head, the slight pressure a warning. Dune pressed her eyes tight as the blindfold was removed. The room was shadowy when she finally blinked her eyes open. She understood then that Lucinda had just shown her her own capacity for sensing beyond what was visible, answering the unasked question.

The first time she came to the Cave she'd wanted to stay. That feeling came again—she wanted to learn from these people whom she had presumed ignorant. The Cave Dwellers were steeped in an awareness that Dune hungered for, awareness of self, awareness of each other and the others, the other forms of life in the space, in the world.

Dune had thought that Mama Rue was her teacher, but she was beginning to understand that it was the common experience of a body being deeply attended to. Paying attention allowed the body to teach all of them.

Lucinda smiled, somehow stepping away before she physically moved. Her voice, a deep and matter of fact Appalachian twang, was at Dune's ear. "You are this place. You don't have to do anything; just by being, the world around you becomes fertile. What you know, the land knows. What you need, the land offers. Bring your feet to the dirt. Bring your face to the bark, bring your blood to the river, bring your rage and your passion to the fire. Bring your heart to the moon. You are a channel of the earth. I love you."

Dune kept her eyes closed, in meditation. She took her time to feel the spilling over of herself into this new assessment, which felt true. She expanded from deep within herself, filling out to the edges. Expanding out into a space of energetic boundary around her, a space she could expand more and more. She felt the synapses of herself deciding to very intentionally be her full size, body and spirit. No more, but no less.

When Dune opened her eyes again, she was alone in the room.

Permission

At dinner the next day, Dune asked Rio if it was ok to bring other people to the Cave. They were at a table alone in the corner, a seat between them as a silent chaperone. Rio seemed to think about it for a second, chewing buttered bread.

"Why are you asking me that?" Rio finally asked, raising an invisible monocle, suspicious.

"Well, you were so intentional about bringing me there."

Rio chuckled then. "That's cause those people worship you, Dune."

Dune chuckled too, slowly realizing Rio was serious. Rio was looking at her like they could see two things concurrently. "They do. *You* know all the ways you did what you did. But to most people here—shoot, to most people in Detroit—you're on a different level."

"Everyone has some kind of magic . . ."

"People say that, but most of us just got a month or two of sharper hearing, or mild telepathy. My homie Zac has, like, less gravity, so, yay a great gift on the basketball court? The best gifts anyone else has are variations on Ajana's listening to plants and trees and stuff, and she is the best by far. And that doesn't come *close* to what you do." Dune was reminded of her magic-mapping project, and suddenly voracious to begin. She was ready.

"I didn't do it alone."

"You say that as if you mean you are collaborating with dead people," Rio smirked. "Not doing shit alone—even that is part of your magic."

"Ok, I know it is special. I do. But it's not like I'm doing something all the time."

"Aren't you though? The wall stays up." Rio gave the half-shrug that meant they'd made their point. "Then you go around singing songs that make people want to live. It's fine, it's a good thing. Most people in Murmur City can be normal around you; we know you're weird and shy, and you just act so normal. But you're also a big deal. Kat and I didn't want you to get mobbed."

Rio reached their bread over and dipped it in Dune's cooling stew before they finished. "Long answer short, you can bring whoever you want. You're a special guest."

Dune's Ancestor Journal, January

we don't know how precious the time is. the whole time, even when we know we are dying, even when we want to live, we don't know.

we don't know when we are in a life moment that will change everything, that will matter. we don't know when we are forming a core memory, not until much later. we forget so much.

we don't know that this person we are opening our heart to will break it. we don't know that this person we are showing our broken heart to could mend it. we don't know it isn't meant to be a grand production of suffering. we don't know how simple a good life is.

we don't know that we are perfect already. we don't know that this is exactly how it's supposed to go, and we don't have to battle for our lives. we don't know that true love always leads to justice.

we don't know who we are. we don't know that everyone else can already see us. we don't know that there is no winning, just fully experiencing.

we don't know much.

Mama Tazina

Mama Tazina said an immediate yes when Dune asked her to go to the Cave.

They met in the dining atrium, Mama Tazina's hair in fresh cornrows that she'd braided herself. They began the walk.

"I've been there before, but the vibes weren't for me," Mama Tazina said, in a tone of playful confession. "I mean I like to process. And do."

Dune almost cackled in a way that didn't feel familiar to her. Mama Tazina made her miss Kama intensely. "I didn't think it was gonna be cool. But it feels really good in there now. I like Kat. Have you met him?"

"Him? Who?"

"The pastor?"

"Ohhh. Mmhmmm, that human right there gives a good word." Mama Tazina reached the door to the Cave first and held it open for Dune. "I am catching up on the gender things, baby."

"Ok, well, catch up quick," Dune awkwardly patted Mama Tazina's arm.

"Anything I should know about you and . . . that?" Mama Tazina glanced down at Dune's outfit—her usual gray joggers, a sweatshirt, crisp white and gray Air Force 1s she'd found in a house that seemed to have been abandoned unexpectedly.

Dune laughed hard. "No." She thought about how intimately

her gender fluidity showed itself and gave Mama Tazina a mischievous look. "Nothing I can imagine telling you."

Mama Tazina wiggled her feral eyebrows. With her storm-white hair and her deep black skin against a bright yellow dress, she looked fresh from ceremony.

In the Cave they found two seats next to each other. The speaker was a burly, bearded, beautiful brown man, with long hair, and massive eyes that moved slowly. He gave the impression that he was deeply present, and listening to something amusing. Dune had never seen him and mimed that to Mama Tazina, just in case he was bad.

"We aren't supposed to know all this." He paused and looked around as if he could have a private moment with each of them. His voice was shaped by another land, which made Dune wonder about his journey to this one. Dune grew up inside such a sharp critique of the US that when she was a child she had asked, "Why does anyone live here? Why don't we all leave?" She had thought the only reasonable immigration was exodus. He continued, "All that out there, we're not supposed to know about it. We know too much and it makes life exhausting."

Eyes closed, bodies rocked. Dune sat with what she had been through, what they had all been through, and how exhausting it was. There had not been rest—there had been change, there had been weeping. There had been dissociating, there had been learning to survive. There had been so much unknown. She wouldn't have remembered it without prompting, but she was exhausted before the virus came. This state was beyond that; what happens when exhaustion is normal.

"We are meant to know about the heartbreaks of our family, our village, that's enough. In a human life, you are supposed to know enough people. But not too many. You need enough to be loved, to be well-friended. To have people to care for and to be taken care of. To have some opposition, someone to begrudge." The room chuckled uncomfortably.

"You don't actually need enemies. You do need inspiration.

"Don't go looking for what to do out in the world. Traveling is good but eventually you realize it's all about finding home, coming home, choosing home. Somebody always needs you at home, including you." The room was about as full as Dune had ever seen it, and people were offering feedback with moans and mmhmms and, "That's right, brother Roush!"

"And! Home is wherever you hold that which holds you." He shared each thought in a dynamic and deliberate way. Then he sat and let the room feel into understanding, pulling on his beard and brushing his fingers through it, rubbing on a high rotund tummy.

Questions

Afterwards, Roush sat in a small room just off the main Cave space. The room had a big pot of the herbal coffee that had become their norm, mismatched mugs and powdered creamer. They were arranged on a table that wobbled to the touch, surrounded by chairs built to be stacked. People came through to visit with him. Dune and Mama Tazina waited in the atrium for a chance to speak with him, mostly because others had, which piqued Mama Tazina's curiosity.

As they waited, they kept their talk too small to interest nearby ears. Dune could now feel the increased attention towards her. She felt amused that she had thought she was stealth before.

When they finally reached him, he looked at them with bright welcome, as if they were his first visitors. They sat at the table, poured themselves coffee. Kat joined them in the kitchen. The conversation was soft at first, a cross-cultural exchange.

Roush and Kat had some kind of swirling tension between them; Dune couldn't quite place it.

Roush would ask a question, "Dune, how did you know to build an altar?"

And Kat would add on, "We heard you had an altar, in your basement."

Roush would interrogate, "Did you back up the files?"

And Kat would add, "We heard you were gathering information about the grievers? Before the wall?"

Dune was measured in her answers, halfway surprised by how much they knew, trying to keep track of what she wanted to share and what she wanted to keep to herself. The house was hers and her family's. The altar was made with her parents' bodies. She'd never shared parts of the story, the whole thing seemed so primal and far away from her mouth, but she also felt that soft invitation to speak that can arise in sacred spaces.

And she had a question to ask them. It was a question she was beginning to want to ask everyone.

"Do you think having the wall around the city is a mistake?"

Everyone got quiet in a different way.

"For who?" Roush finally asked, a benevolent smile on his lips.

Dune was confused. "For us, for the people who live here."

Roush chuckled and looked around at the others in the room. "But we didn't make the wall. It can't be a mistake for us."

"Do you mean, do we think you made a mistake?" Kat was asking gently, his hands, delicate and poised.

"Yes." Dune was counting breaths in her head, trying to find the pace of this exchange.

"Why did you do it?" Roush asked, as if the choice were merely intriguing and not in any way related to his life.

Mama Tazina intervened, "Who taught her otherwise?"

"I didn't say it was wrong. But intentions do matter. The possibility of mistake is impossible to measure without intent," Roush spoke like a shrug.

"Protection. I just wanted to stop them. I wanted to create safety."

Kat nodded and placed a hand on Dune's. "It's never a mistake to move towards safety. It doesn't mean there won't be new dangers, different problems. But the amount of traumatic death we all witnessed back there? Most of the community doesn't deal with it. Some days I walk around almost feeling like we spontaneously created a little utopia—not as a reaction to genocide, but because it was fun. Which isn't fucking true."

"Well, what's true is that what happened is in the past," Roush was stroking his beard in a way that made Dune want one. It looked to her like he had created a pet that needed no care, just petting and stroking all day long. "We are merely human. One way we survive is to forget and seek the normalcy available to us, the small good."

What's wrong with a little utopia? Dune wondered. She thought about the men, the ones who had dreamt up H-8 and unleashed it on her city. She confessed, "I'm not good. I'm not good like you. I can't stop wishing death upon those men. I can't shake it off."

The room shifted here, recentering around the expressed violence from Dune. She instantly wished she could pull the words back.

"Does that mean the wall is also a weapon?" Kat asked, clumsily. "Does it kill people who try to cross?"

Dune's body tucked in around her heart. She should know this answer and she had no idea. "I don't think so. We can ask Ajana." At their blank stares, she added, "One of our seers. Do you have a lot of people with active magic here?"

"Is the wall protecting them?" Roush felt impenetrable, rejecting her pivot. He was holding Dune's gaze somehow. "Protecting 'those men' from the death in you?"

She couldn't speak for a moment, so surprised by the feeling of attack. She felt ashes under her nails, in the crevices of her palms. It was hard to breathe, and she didn't want to be here. Mama Tazina closed the distance between their chairs and put a hand on Dune's thigh.

Dune briefly went rigid, unwilling to show any more to this group of strangers. She caught Kat's eye and he looked concerned. She intentionally made her face softer, unreadable, noncombative. Dune turned back to Roush, "Perhaps. Thank you for letting me witness your service. Really moving," She let herself mean it. "We have to head back."

She stood up, as Roush smiled over his surprise—and was he offended? He offered his hand. She fist-bumped him, some instinct wanting to avoid his open palm against hers. She and Mama Tazina were quiet until the elevator doors closed behind them.

Cheetah-fast, Mama Tazina grabbed Dune and pulled her tight against her chest, hands pressing into her back, a lifeguard checking for breath. Dune took a moment to thaw into trust. Then she spit curses against Mama Tazina's shoulder, grabbing onto the elder's sweater, needing to punch something. There were no tears, but so much rage. By the time they stepped off the elevator, Dune had composed herself.

Mama Tazina paused and faced Dune directly. "Baby. You don't have to justify your magic to him or any other man. They killed *your mother*. You will have to harness that rage for your highest good and highest work. But first you must feel it. If they had done nothing else, they killed your mother."

Dune nodded, feeling a storm in her chest, a nausea of the heart. She decided to ask Berta to help her find a way to release it.

Senses

Dog
The human who grew the city is learning to feel.

She is listening to the humans who listen, she is following the humans who follow. She is singing songs that already exist, but only on the wind, until they move through the right instrument.

She is learning, in all of these ways, to feel what we feel, the interconnected world, the world of the senses and the relationships.

Marta by the Wall
Marta had found an abandoned apartment near the wall to squat, and every day she drove back to observe a different segment of the border. What Marta learned from sitting in her car outside the wall:

1. People were trying to get in the wall, through it. Every day, people chopped and cut at the wall, getting nowhere. She watched

a group of young men douse the base of the wall with something out of a red canister and throw matches into it, producing a small fire, and still no impact on the wall.

2. A world was growing around the wall—there were people camping by the wall, living up against it, creating systems of barter and trade amongst themselves. Especially on the north side up by Grosse Pointe, life on the wall almost felt normal.

3. There was no capacity to control the wall community—this was one of many concurrent crises in the world. There were signs intended to keep people farther away, but no real enforcement, just a handful of people with no uniform, giving warnings and driving off.

4. The people making their lives near and around the wall had no doubt that there were people still alive inside. When Marta moved amongst them, trying to understand their basis for this belief, she discovered love stories, tales of faith, and a deep well of hopeful feelings that were fed by signs and patterns. She felt the dissonance of doubting these methods while already being of these people, outside the wall, pulled by her own love and faith and something in her gut.

5. Thousands of white Detroiters had died by suicide after evacuating the city in the wake of H-8. The jury was out on the correlation between H-8 exposure and these deaths—were they chemical reactions, or guilt? The world was in such a state of global chaos and conflict that there wasn't nearly enough attention being paid to this longer-form danger of the virus. Or to Detroit at all. There was a misinformation campaign that claimed there had only been a few survivor's-guilt suicides, and the numbers were being grossly exaggerated in order to deter copycat attacks of H-8. But Marta slowly realized that most of the white

people around her were desperate to get back into the city before a suicidal urge took them.

Berta

Dune's anger was a palpable energy in her. She shared with Berta what had happened in the Cave, how defensive she had felt, how misunderstood, how scared. Berta had Dune bicycle her heels against the massage table, one at a time, pushing down with as much pressure as she could handle. Soon Dune was sweating, a strangled sound in her throat.

"Would you try one other thing with me?" Berta asked, gentle. She stood Dune up and placed a broomstick, twisted free of its head, into Dune's hands. She walked her over to the twin bed where she often encouraged her clients to rest after sessions. Berta modeled for Dune a way to raise the broomstick up over her head and drop it down, bending her knees, letting gravity land the impact on the bed. Dune did this once, then twice, and then countless times, screaming and beating the world that had frightened her so, taken so much from her. She beat the bed until she collapsed onto it, panting and spent, face wet with tears and spit.

As Dune caught her breath, Berta quietly asked, "What do you know, now?"

Dune spoke between gulps of air, "From the moment my mother began dying, and then when the bodies were everywhere . . . all of that came into me, like into a bottomless well that somehow feels bloated . . . and there was no way back out. There were things I saw that I should not have seen . . . and I needed a way to get them out. Binging guarantees a purge, a way to get it out of me. Binging always feels like a treat. Purging feels like the appropriate cost. I didn't know it was spiritual work. I didn't know there were other ways to do it that might feel better."

Berta rubbed a hand down her back and hummed, giving Dune room to rest in the release and to integrate the wisdom. "Leave it here. We can keep emptying that well whenever you need to."

Paris

Dune was beginning to understand that sitting alone in the Cave was calming for her. When she looked around with clear eyes, the space looked like the rest of the building: institutional, bland, carpeted, with strange gray patterns on the walls. But the Cave was not about what one could see. Softening her eyes, Dune could always feel that the room was steeped with prayer, spirit visitors, a thickness that felt good in the way resting into a needed hug feels good.

Today a few strangers preceded her, and Lucinda was in the far corner, deep in her own quiet. Dune found a seat far from the others and closed her eyes, letting her thoughts wander.

She had asked Hoka to put her on the Mbongi Council agenda for next week and she was slowly drafting up a process for documenting the magics of Murmur City to present to them.

She missed things being easy with Dawud.

She missed things being allowed with Rio.

She missed Kama, who would have nosed her way into all of it.

She thought about the wall, which was doing another magical transition—as the leaves fell off of it, evergreen pine needles took their place. When this had happened the first winter, Dune had to remind herself that it wasn't a familiar act of nature. It was something beyond that. Dune knew that, even now, there were people attending to how and why the wall worked. But there were things she could only do if she didn't try to understand them.

Dune heard someone sit behind her. She could hear steady breathing, and smell something that triggered a memory from childhood... standing eye level at a grown woman's vanity, a scent of white amber, a massive puff in a container of scented powder. Dune, back in the now, peeked over her shoulder. A glamorous Creole woman sat behind her, older but also ageless, a red lip, a fascinator with a cloud of silvery mesh perched on top of her up-do. Milky black skin with constellations of freckles and moles, each well placed.

"I miss places more than people. I miss Paris." The stranger's voice was quiet, feminine and nonchalant in a way her eyes contradicted. She spoke in the crisp, lilted affect of Black people who know no one is superior to them. No one else in the space spoke and Dune didn't think she should either, so she just nodded, bringing Paris to mind.

Dune's own travel memories were dusty, sepia, full of playing on the edges of circles in which her parents discussed the problems and solutions of the world with global comrades, not traversing sights or even tasting local cuisine. Brendon and Kama had generally oriented towards the immigrant food wherever they were—Surinamese in Amsterdam, Mexican on the Canadian border, Italian in Ghana, Senegalese in Paris—delicious and often more affordable.

"It's like having babies—nonono then miraculous yessss," the woman continued. "The whole time I'm there I'm bruised by the tiny planes, slipping down those shallow stairs, feet freezing in the bathrooms—the conquering barbarians don't even heat their bathrooms! And, of course, wounded by the racism. That's one birthplace of hatred. And the violations are immense. But then the pain au chocolat of it all lands, and you lick the croissant flakes from your lip, smoke Gauloises and write for hours on end, steam at the Arab baths, sing at the queerest Black salon, drag a new lover through a chic crowd to see Venus and Mona. And you depart and you say, 'I should live here, I'm going to live here one year.'"

Her expression didn't change from a soft, raw smile. But something deep in the lines of her face deepened as a tragic wave moved inside her.

"Only now it doesn't seem like I will. And I didn't know that was the last time."

The woman closed her eyes and lowered her head. Dune looked away for the briefest moment, to gather some comfort. When she turned to face the elder, the woman was gone, only the scent of her remained on the air. Dune turned and turned, darting her eyes into every corner, through the glass doors.

Was this a new level of ancestral interaction? A threat? A warning? A madness? Dune didn't get to revel in it because Sahari was walking across the Cave towards her. Her cheeks were soft again, her head wrapped in white cotton, she wore a simple, square white dress. She tilted her head to the hallway, an invitation.

They stood facing each other, outside the door, where anyone could witness.

"Snitch," Sahari said, lightly, smirking a bit.

Dune was caught off guard and laughed, "You feeling better?"

"It's all relative for me," Sahari smiled. Dune was stuck once again by how dazzling her beauty was, how bright. "I've been sleeping well here. Eating every day. You're looking good too."

Dune looked down at herself. Her body didn't feel different, but she noticed for the first time that she hadn't binged since the day Rio had found Sahari, overdosed. She'd been to the gym more often, strength training. Sahari's dance with death had left Dune wanting to feel her body, wanting her life. But none of this felt appropriate to share, so she just said "thank you."

"Thank you, Dune." Sahari's eyes searched hers and Dune still felt mystery in Sahari's gaze, even danger. "I am here and I know you're a part of that."

Dune stayed quiet for a moment, waiting for something true to arise. "I'm glad you're here."

"It's not personal, you and I." Sahari looked down. Dune could feel something dissipate between them. Dune offered her hand. Sahari looked at it for a moment and then took it.

"I'm Dune. Dune Chen."

Sahari smiled at her, fragile and open. "Sahari Hendrix."

Dune's Ancestor Journal, January

my family lived in my body, in my time. most of em came through me into the world and at the end of each day i folded them back into myself to give them a place where they could leave whatever the world had carved into them, whatever projections they had endured:

the bus ride
cleaning their shoes
ferrying them around town
serving them whiskey neat
carrying their children out the mud
(every Black person you know been raised a white person up)
my husband needed the most rescue. he was a holy man, so he was

full of such deep rage. he brought it into my body during that time—
this was how we kept them out the jail:
   letting them pour all the horrors into our ears
   letting them pour that fury inside us
   letting them treat us like a place that would never collapse, sturdy
beyond structure.
   the plates broke on my walls. the bullets caught in my teeth.
   the children slept peacefully. the husband slept peacefully.
   i never slept.
   there was praying to do.
   i was a house.

Dune sat still, feeling the house of her own body. Then she wrote back, for the first time.

"Please come to me this way, not like that lady. It's too vulnerable for me to receive in that way, especially in public. This is the safest way." She sat back and felt into the energy of the room. She always felt both confident in the magical impulses, and a bit silly as she did them. But before long, she felt an acceptance of her boundary spell, a soft rightness all around her.

A house has walls.

Portal

It was during the working of a spell that a new, wildly unexpected, kind of portal opened between Dune and Mama Rue.

The two women were sitting across a circle, holding worlds and a few generations between them. They were guiding what Mama Rue had called a Wholing Ceremony, to allow spiritual gold to pour into a heartbroken place—a lover had gone missing, and the beloved was asking the community to help draw him home, connect the community to his heart.

Dune often had the sense that Mama Rue would merge into the people that she served. The small moments of joy, empathy, sanity, and connection that reached Mama Rue's face all came at the conclusion of a ritual. And this time, as Mama Rue channeled the prayers of the room, she suddenly reached a place of peace so deep that Dune could feel it move as a wave, around the circle and through her, from both directions. The whole circle was tethered between their bodies, and though they both had their eyes closed, Dune felt like something in her could see that they were both beings of light, beyond time, beyond flesh.

When the ceremony ended, her awareness of the light beam truth of them wouldn't fully dissipate and she ended up quietly walking Mama Rue home and following her inside. She could see Mama Rue pulsing, the light beating darker and darker as they stood there, Dune at Mama Rue's back.

Finally, Dune stepped forward and wrapped herself around Mama Rue, left cheek pressed into her soft 'fro, both hands cupping Mama Rue's belly. She willed her own energy into a cool, soft, blue light, and poured it through every inch of her that touched her teacher. Mama Rue was briefly stiff, almost pulling away. Then she was soft and leaning back into Dune's arms. Dune knew, as if holding her own body, that it had been too long since Mama Rue had been held and touched as a woman. Dune turned Mama Rue towards her and just held her deeply, kissing her shining forehead and feeling all the life and power that Mama Rue walked with. And then, holding each other hip to hip in this hallway, the women let their energies completely merge. It was the kind of lesbian merging that Dune had missed since Marta left and Rio took sex off the table. It was also a togetherness unlike anything Dune had known, a complete release of any individual impulse, a total surrender to the connection. Their bodies scarcely moved, micro undulations. But their energy bodies rushed all over, in every direction at once. Their breathing and eventually the chorus of pleasure sounds filling the space became the physical proof of what was moving between and because of them.

The climax was one prayer uttered through two bodies; the women collapsed against each other and the closest wall.

When Dune opened her eyes, she saw the woman Rue, face unguarded in its pleasure. Rue's eyes were mischievous, powerful, direct, and soft, a fire burning steady without drama. Rue leaned up and kissed Dune on the cheek. "Thank you. I needed that."

Dune giggled, feeling such ease and rightness in this moment, no thought of anything before or after. "Me too."

It wasn't until she was almost at dinner that she paused and felt a small panic—how would she explain this to Dawud? To Rio? To anyone?

Spirit Bang

"So you spirit banged your teacher?" Dawud chuckled, but sharply.

Dune held her tongue.

"Girl, I can't keep up with you. *She's never satisfied.*" His tone was light, but she could feel a new texture of hurt in him.

"It was unexpected—and it wasn't about desire, not really. It was about connection."

Dawud was shaking his head. He was in the window seat on the east side of their space, facing the city that contained them.

Dune was leaning against the kitchen counter, trying to pull solidity from the granite. She knew she hadn't done anything wrong, but some part of her still felt guilty. She wanted Dawud to be excited with her for this experience, which felt like an evolution. But they were just getting their sexual rhythm back after Captain's death and Dune's exposed disordered eating, and the battle of the wall. Now he felt like a brick barricade in front of her, no doors, no windows.

"Look, it's fine. We open, do your thing." He turned his face towards her, and she could see the struggle in him, the desire to be fine vs the truth of how hurt he was.

"Baby, Rue is not a threat to you. To us."

Dawud nodded, picking up the pillow behind him and adjusting it. "Not Mama anymore, huh?"

"No. I see her as a person, as a woman, as an energy. She has been giving so much for so long and, like . . . She hasn't been held. She hasn't had the kind of intimacy that makes all this huge spirit shit sustainable."

Dawud's face softened a bit. "Dune . . . she's crazy crazy. And Rio is . . . unavailable. And I am not them."

Dune felt confused and let it show. Dawud continued, "I'm not a woman . . . an old woman in need of sexual favor or a young desirable stud—that's what they have in common. I'm not what you want. I'm not."

Dune was stretched in so many directions—wanting to comfort her lover, wanting to be true to what had happened with Rue, which wasn't an act of charity or insanity. Dune felt the reach of the experiment that she and Dawud were always up to, swimming upstream with each other, against their own natures. "I know who you are, Dawud. I just feel like I have found a new part of who I am."

"This part isn't fun." Dawud looked like a stranger in his body. "I want to just be chill about this, but it feels like . . . so much."

The light shifted through the window and within Dune. She walked towards him, and Dawud opened his legs to make room for her; their bodies moved into the familiar shape of holding each other. Dune tucked into the bowl of Dawud's lap, and she leaned back against him.

"You're exactly what I want, Dawud."

They both felt the lie in that sentence, but neither could understand where it was rooted.

He spoke against her ear, "I know we're gay. I know you need women, I need men, I know that. And I like our transgressive shit. But now you're fucking in some alternate spirit realm that I don't even understand? Like, you like having me around, yes. I take out the trash, I kill the bugs, yes. But," Dawud pressed his face against her hair, voice near a whisper, "I'm not some magical woman."

Dune smiled, tender. She nuzzled her head back against his mouth. "Dawud B. Don't diminish yourself. You've always been you, since we met. And I have loved you almost every day since then." They both gave a small laugh at that. "I love you. Nothing that happens with other people changes us. It might change those other relationships. But we good."

Dawud shook his head. He knew what she didn't: that everything changed everything else, in a million small, sand-shifting ways. Right now she didn't know it, but she was already different. She loved him, sure, but the novelty that truly kept her loyal to him, that was elsewhere now, and they were forever changed.

Prophecy

The Cave

On her next trip into the Cave of the Heart, Dune brought Dawud. She told him she wanted him to assess the safety and sanity of the community there, which was mostly true. She also wanted to not be apart, for him to feel her constancy. And she wanted him to see Lucinda, or more accurately, she thought the seer might have something to teach him. She felt nervous about crossing Roush's path again, but she was more prepared. She didn't want him to keep her from this place, these people. She suspected that some relationship between Murmur City and the people of the Cave was crucial for understanding what needed to happen with the wall.

Since Dune's spirit bang with Rue, Dawud had been a bit further away, inside himself. Dune hoped it would pass soon. She wasn't even sure if she and Rue would cross that line again; they hadn't spoken of it. Dawud felt less vivid, less gregarious, as they walked into the dark center of Murmur City.

The room only had a few people in it, but Kat and Lucinda were amongst them. They all seemed to be meditating, so Dune and Dawud sat towards the back and settled into the quiet. Eventually, Kat's soft voice nudged the room into collective company. He asked if anyone had a request or something to offer. No one spoke up, so he gently let everyone go, waving at Dune to bring Dawud up to where he and Lucinda were sitting.

As Dune introduced everyone, she got to see Lucinda have a young, girly moment. Dawud B was famous even here. Dune, surprised, thought that the seer might be too dazzled to help Dawud in this moment. She was about to initiate a polite exit when Lucinda and Dawud's eyes closed at the same time.

Dawud's face went soft in the candlelight, tilting back in a way Dune recognized from the radio show. Then he did some new things—his hands opened, palms up, wide, cloud-catching. Lucinda's did the same. His mouth was smiling and then he was speaking.

". . . In the same way the bees and flowers have a symbiosis at the level of design, so do humans with this Earth. But the part you do not include or understand is time. There is a specific time for every seduction. Every fertilization. Every loss, every change.

"Time is not linear but constant and coexistence all at once. Some can move amongst times, arrange things inside of time, in their waking or dreaming.

"Ah my love, constriction is a construct . . . you have been growing your whole life in just the phase of bursting open a seed and pushing out through the dirt. Are you ready to go up, into the spacious realm above ground? Or are you mycelial in nature, only needing the sun third hand?

"The awakening of powers comes from breaking through beyond the dirt.

"There is a purpose in the seed that falls to the wayside, even in the lives that seem to fail or be lost. There is a purpose to each breathing body and each pebble and each wild creature.

"Death is not less gorgeous than life. It is your limitation on understanding how grand love is . . .

"This is not the first maroon space. Most of the Earth is a pattern of spaces made sacred by the grief they hold. Why you think the swamp so thick?"

Then he was singing an unfamiliar song in soothing baritone, "They return as elements of nature / as trees, as birds / as everything wi-iii-ild / go outside, go outside."

He opened his eyes and found Dune, grabbing her hands and searching her face for understanding. He looked like both himself and a stranger. "You're right, they're all here baby. We become intensely powerful in the spirit realm when we die from injustice. Some of that becomes vengeful—it's why so few privileged people are at peace or happy. But if those of us on this side practice, we can harness and use the power to advance our justice work, our boundaries."

Dawud swayed a bit then, looking disoriented, dizzy. He looked around himself and then lay down on the bench and fell asleep. Lucinda's eyes opened and she exhaled deeply.

"What a gift," she said to Kat and Dune. "What an incredible gift."

Dune's Ancestor Journal, February

but the closer you are to the norm, the harder it is to feel free of it. i imagine i would have suffered so much more if i had been born with "light" skin, "seductive" eyes, "good" hair, or god forbid, been skinny. there would be an expectation that i would rest in whatever beauty i had and keep trying to make it better, closer, more perfect. i would live my life as a presentation of my incredible beauty. ha! no, i knew early, in school days, that there was no way around it. i was ugly: my nose hinting of altercation, my eyes a bit too small to get lost in, my mouth turned slightly downward when i was thinking, and i was always thinking. i was shaped like a human, not an hourglass or a pear or a mannequin. beauty was never part of my appeal, so i developed what i did get. i'm the smartest person in any room i enter. smart as in quick witted. smart as in well studied. smart as in i can deduce the conclusion before you. i always have a lover because i'm good company and i'm as smart about pleasure as i am about everything else. the norm was never an option for me, not for one day. now you think i'm bold and brave, but i promise you it was my only option. it took a long, long time to relinquish envy, but i've mostly done it now. i don't envy the journey you're on now—you've always been light skinned and pretty and skinny, even if you lacked any feminine charm. now you are learning to be fat, which in this society has generally been a kind of ugly, though there are pockets of humanity where that's shifting. you will decide if it's just a grief visitation state or feels like who you are now. your body is fine. it's just your mind, it's all in your mind, it's all going to be determined in your mind.

Dune finished journaling and started laughing. "Ok y'all. Ok." She set the journal to the side, feeling unexpected completion—she had somehow caught up to the present moment, even with her ghosts. It was time to focus on magic.

Sun

"There is a change you go through, most of us women do, where you no longer want to hide any of your desires. You want to wear them on your skin. You want it to be the first thing people see when they look at you—I am overflowing with desire." Rue was looking at herself in the mirror that sat at the end of her bed, lioness eyes and hair. Her rooms were a mixture of patterns so abundant that Dune couldn't tell if the blankets and curtains were collages or layers. There was so much to see in every direction.

Rue was coiled up on the end of her bed, naked, one leg crossed over the other, foot dangling. "Almost every woman I know awakens into her massive sexual beloved self and she wants to be wanted, tasted, seduced, touched, known. Very few women actually get any kind of satisfying experience of this, it is almost always too brief, or in some way compromised. You can have love if you share it. You can have it if you'll tolerate dishonesty. You can have it from a fool. You can have it from someone who can't handle intimacy.

"Or, it never happens. No one ever looks at you deeply, no one wants what they see, no one falls in love with your heart. I have always been mad, and I have always been sexy, so I have always had lovers, while sane women looked on, sucking their teeth. I have made such good love to so many people. But so long ago. Age is the only thing you can't cover with a great performance. It's non-negotiable."

Rue turned her face in the mirror, tilted her shoulders, as if she wanted to see behind herself and all around.

"You've had such sweet romantic love, actually. You don't know. I know. I know what it's like to share a home with someone who is slowly killing you in a way that can't be proven. I know what it's like to love someone who will never love themselves. I know what it's like to offer someone your whole heart every day, but they can't stop looking for something new and so, of course, neither can you. I lived in an era just below love. I think history will realize that. The heartbreak generation; living long enough to see the realization of love's potential in relationships amongst their children, the loss too familiar to relinquish. I am not bitter about it anymore. We live when we live and some of it is crisis.

"Thank you for whatever little gift this is, though. You lend me sweetness. I never thought . . . I thought it was a part of my life that had died prematurely. Now so much life is just pouring straight through me."

"You are a clear channel," Dune noticed, sprawled across the bed behind Rue, catching her eye in the mirror. They had laid here for over an hour, merging. Dune believed she knew everything knowable about Rue, the way she knew herself. She had examined the purest aspects of this intimate teacher.

Rue rocked back, finding her tailbone playfully, almost losing balance a few times before softening all the way into Dune's pillow belly. "I don't stay like this. Don't fall in love."

Dune smiled, "You taught me something a while ago. Form follows function. That the healing we do is a function in direct response to the need in nature, the need in people, the wounds. I need something, you need something; it takes this form now."

Rue was still watching herself in the mirror. "Yes," she affirmed, "and then it will shift."

Dune pulled Rue against her like a child. "And then it will shift."

Mbongi Council

Dune was finally ready to present to the Mbongi Council.

Hoka was guiding the council now through a conversation on how to access a wider variety of meat than the fish and chicken they were cultivating. There weren't a ton of cows, pigs, or goats in the city, and they would need to breed the existing livestock for a few years to begin to generate enough meat to cover regular meals. They had found so many chicken coops in the city, with both broilers and laying hens, but most of the other livestock was beyond the wall, unreachable. Hoka asked if there was anyone willing to do some research and bring a proposed timeline for generating a regular source of meat. Vincent, the young Chinese man who had been appointed into Dune's vacant spot, took on the task.

What was supposed to be next on the agenda was an issue having to do with the carpets throughout Murmur City, which were a constant, glaring reminder that their home had been a hotel and conference center not too long ago. Dune was curious about where all the spirits woven into the carpets would go. Hoka changed paths before they could get into the conversation, noting that Dune was in attendance and they should honor her time. Dune tried to look grateful.

There was no graphic or image or thing to present to the council and as she waited for her agenda item, Dune had started to feel a bundle of odd nerves—discussing other people's ideas was different from presenting her own. Hoka's jump scare agenda moves worked as an intervention. All eyes were on Dune.

"I am excited to begin to map the magic of Murmur City," Dune started. "Some people became very . . . magical, in response to H-8. Which we all know." She took a deep breath and noticed her feet on the ground, squared her shoulders and placed a hand just under her belly button. She reminded herself this was just twelve people in a small pocket of the whole world, none of them strangers. The only thing new was that she was openly discussing magic, hers and others.

"Some of that magic has faded, but we don't currently have any way of understanding who we are and what we are capable of. So, I want to create a Magic Map that allows us to understand how many people have some degree of magical capacity, and record audio of the interviews I have with people. I want to hear about people's magic in their own words and from there we can see if there are patterns... Like, Ajana's magic and mine feel connected, but they are distinct, so I can observe the pattern but I won't name anything until I have more data. I'd like to set up a space in Wind Tower where people can come and be interviewed with some degree of privacy, and I'll add them to the map. I think about six months will give me time to hear from everyone who is interested in sharing. It might be slow, there might also be people who don't know their magic, but this should be a good start."

The council asked a few questions. Ed wanted to know if she had a list of necessary supplies (not yet), Ajana asked if she needed help (probably). The council's response was quick and positive, and Mohamed said he would work on finding her a space to work. She was trying to decide if she could just slip out or if she had to stay the duration of the meeting, when Hoka cleared her throat. "Dune, there is one more question we have, which feels related."

Dune felt a small grip in her gut. "What's up?"

Hoka looked around at the council, as if maybe one of them would speak. They mostly all looked at Dune or out windows and at walls. Hoka pursed her lips just enough to let Dune know that whatever was coming wasn't something that originated with her.

"We have been having some discussion about the wall. It's very clear to everyone here why the wall was created. It is very unclear how it was created and if we have any agency over our future when it comes to this barrier. We have been in here now coming on three years. Mohamed's team has been making some breakthroughs with internet access—Mohamed can you briefly explain what you have accomplished?"

Mohamed nodded, a slight crinkle at his eyes showing his excitement. "With Dawud's help we basically found a way to access internet. We have had the mesh network and that's really been incredible for internal communications, but for security purposes it felt important to have a way to observe what's happening beyond our boundary. In the Observation Room there is now what we call Total Perspective—we can see the water, we can observe the boundary, and we can observe the world beyond the boundary, and our skies which, for now, are clear."

Dune felt surprisingly uninterested in the world beyond their boundary, but she was glad there were people thinking about security.

"We have so much information on what's happening, but there is a growing desire to truly understand this wall and our relationship to it. And it feels like you and Ajana are the ones with magic that can help us understand the wall. In addition to mapping other people's magic, we would love to have a better sense of yours."

Dune felt like she was about to be assigned an unwanted partner.

"One question we have, to which you may not know the answer, is—can the wall come down? If you wanted it to?" Hoka leaned forward a bit.

Dune looked carefully at the faces looking at her. While there was no visible malice, there was some tenderness and she realized that they had . . . strategized. About bringing this to her. She looked at Ed to verify—yes, he was clearly pressing his mouth shut under some predetermined instruction to not mess this up. This made her feel wary and curious, until she let the question really land in her. "I told Dawud I would try to figure out what I could do with the wall. It's not easy . . . it doesn't feel like a sound decision."

Before Hoka could answer, Mama Tazina was speaking. "Baby, some of us have family out there. Some of us just here 'cause we were grieving so tough we couldn't imagine leaving, but we healing. Some of us just don't like how it happened, that there was no collective process. Most of us want to be right here, doing this—we recognize what a precious opportunity this is, to find a way for humans to be on Earth together . . . but we human, baby. We nomadic."

Ajana spoke up next, "Also, it would just be cool to know what's possible. The plants that become part of a wall are not as clear to me, like I don't know their right name. We could know so much more about what's happening on our perimeter. Maybe the wall plants might talk to you."

Dune nodded, feeling something rigid in her soften. The impulse to question the wall wasn't *against* her, it was just . . . human. It was just humans having different needs and opinions and processes. People had family outside this city; people needed beef. And it wouldn't hurt to just know what was possible.

"I see. Would it be ok if Ajana interviewed me about my magic? I think that would help me figure out what I do and don't know, because a lot of this has just never really occurred to me." That was as honest as Dune could be with these people. She didn't want to say she didn't know, something about that felt too vulnerable.

"That's a great first step, Dune." Hoka nodded and the topic was complete. Ajana smiled at Dune, as did a few of her friends around the table. But she could feel the presence of other reactions, of unspoken tensions, in this room and amongst unknown numbers of people across this city. People wanting more, faster, different answers from her.

Magics

Solo

Dune stood, wand in hand, in front of the tree that held her home, humbled. It was sunrise; she'd wanted some privacy. She could probably ask the council to set up a security perimeter around this area for her, but she wasn't sure yet if this was the best place from which to communicate with the wall and didn't want to disrupt the sacred ritual practices so many Detroiters did here.

Dawud, and maybe everyone else, wanted the wall down despite all the danger and uncertainty. She wasn't sure she could bring it down, especially because she didn't want to.

She gathered some items from the ground—lost branches, dry leaves, a rock. She arranged them in a semicircle, open towards the tree. She sat behind this altar, holding her wand in both hands, eyeing the tree, feeling ignored. She tried to remember the basement, that feeling of mysterious certainty with which she had known what to do. She felt none of that now.

The tree, which had grown over and under the earth to connect and protect the city, called to Dune. She tucked her wand into her waistband and placed her hands on the bark. She immediately felt how alive it was, how much energy was pulsing in every direction. A million times the force of her wand. This tree, this wall, was so much more powerful than her.

She couldn't bring it down alone, even if she wanted to. Dune had created a solution that made sense to her and all she felt was gratitude. Living without the wall didn't make any sense to her. To take the risk of bringing down the wall would require a ritual, a collective of people, infused with the trust of the community, all doing magic and believing it was the right move. And in the same way there was an offering of body, of pleasure, of prayer, of need, there would need to be an offer made to the wall, a sacrifice, a letting go. The ritual would need to include the offer.

Leaning against the tree now, pressing her ear against the bark, Dune heard music. Not the way it usually came, words and melody flowing. This was a song she couldn't sing alone. Guided by her gut, she pulled the wand out and held it up to her ear. It was there too, a sound of choir and mass celebration moving through her mind and body, swinging back and forth, low and steady, building up into beauty and ecstasy. There was no wall—there was a choir. There was a cacophony. There was a way.

Weaving

Without realizing it, Dune began searching for the spirit in each of her lovers. The way Rue could meld with her on the level of spirit created a unique layer in her orgasms, a sense of connection. She had something akin to memory, a shadowy impression that this sensual spirit had been present before, with lovers she loved.

She tried with Rio, sitting across a table from her. She extended her energy until it was touching Rio. She had the sense that with a slight pressure, she would be flowing through Rio. But Rio jolted and looked up straight at Dune, eyes dark and direct. Their eyebrows asked the question, and Dune flushed and dropped her gaze in response. Until that moment, Dune hadn't considered their boundaries. She dropped her energy, as if it were tentacles that could fall to the floor before she drew them back. Right now Rio was helping Sahari come back to life, though she said they were broken up. Dune would never violate Rio's boundaries, however impatient she felt. The fact that Rio had felt her inquiry was hopeful, she left it at that.

Later that day, kissing Dawud, Dune extended her energy to him through her lips, through her hands. He moaned, instantly more excited. She could feel his energy moving all around and through both of them—wild, no direction, no intention, but fully present. He was kissing her neck, unbuttoning her shirt, and Dune flowed her energy into his. He caught her eye, he knew something was different. She felt him give her permission, she felt him open to her at the same moment he opened her thighs and slid his hands down the front of her pants. Once he moved his palm against her, she stopped trying to control her energy or the boundary between them. Their energies flowed together and centered down into their connected bodies.

Dawud's eyes were on hers when he came, laughing and crying. Dune came shortly after, an exquisite explosion from deep within her being out to the edges of the universe. Dune felt the pleasure through every level of her body and, in that moment, she understood that the cosmic shift of this kind of orgasm was good for the universe.

Later, Dune lay awake, scholarly. She had accumulated three lovers, without really meaning to. The one she was most likely to bed down was the one she couldn't touch, although she felt that, as long as they were both alive, they would be lovers, regardless of the language or limitations. The one she hadn't thought of as an option was turning her out. And the one she would have thought of as the opposite of her desire felt like a part of her body.

This "spirit bang" with Dawud wasn't the same as the pleasure with Rue, that skillful deployment of energy beyond what their bodies could do. This felt wild, possibly dangerous, but she no longer wanted to be touched without the flow of energy.

Ajana

Ajana sat in Dune's living room, shuffling a tarot deck she'd pulled out of a box with Lineages of Change written across the cover in goldleaf.

"What's that for?" Dune asked, bringing water for each of them.

"I've been figuring out some things about my gift. I'm not—"

"Wait," Dune's hands went up, "Can we start recording?"

"Sure, of course." They looked at each other for a moment. Dune hadn't set any parameters or structure for Ajana's interview of her, so it wasn't clear who would do the recording. Dune wanted to be interviewed first, to feel what it was like to be in this seat before she constructed her questions and format, even before she set up the space. Ajana giggled and showed her hands, all she'd brought was the tarot deck and a notebook. Dune dashed off to grab the fancy recorder Dawud had loaned her.

Once she hit record, Dune pointed at Ajana. "Ok, so first I could just 'hear' plants, right, see what they had seen? But then I started to notice a sense of . . . knowing things. Knowledge being available, even when I wasn't touching a plant. I realized, like, I am a living thing dependent on the sun, I am a living seed. Cool. I started knowing more than anyone would want me to. But you can't just walk around saying things at people or they think you're . . ." Ajana made her hands move around her head like a solar system. "Basically, Mama Rue gave me this tarot deck cause she said it helps to focus the knowledge that's coming through. Focus on what's needed in the moment."

"That's interesting." Dune felt the presence of Kama, who loved shit like tarot cards. "Do you ask questions to the tarot?"

"It works however you want it to. Today I only have one question: what does the world need to know about Dune's magic? And the cards will guide me to the right areas."

Dune swallowed her skepticism and centered herself with a few breaths. She relinquished control as Ajana shuffled the cards, humming a bit under her breath. Dune wondered if Ajana also had some of the healing song gift.

Ajana held the deck in her right hand and hovered her left hand over it, slowly pulling one card at a time until she had laid out five cards, face down. She turned over the first one: Death. Ajana looked up at Dune, eyebrows high.

"Ok, Death, the card of ultimate transformation. What role does death play in your gifts?" Ajana was shook, but pressing through.

Dune sat for a minute, trying to think about it. Nothing was clear. She opened her mouth. "I . . . I didn't feel any need for magic until my mom died." She felt grief leap to her throat, familiar. "She was the magic one, she always thought everything was possible, somehow. If you couldn't see the way, then you needed an altar, or a prayer, or a spell, or more people. Her ashes have been a part of any land magic I've ever done. And my mom loved to sing. She didn't think she was good at it, but she said it was necessary. Singing, feeling a song inside and letting it out, is necessary. So maybe I only have my mother's gifts."

Dune felt surprised by her own answers, and a chill. She felt Kama's presence stronger than ever. Ajana nodded, solemn and satisfied. She turned over the next card, Ten of Swords. She grimaced a bit. "And suffering, impossible despair, and hardship?"

Dune was nauseous.

"H-8 forced us to do impossible things. I had to drag my mother and grandmother into the backyard and burn them. I walked through my city when it was covered in more death and bodies than any system could keep up with. I found a way to survive by breaking into my neighbors' homes. I knew shit was corrupt, but I didn't believe how bad it could get. No, I didn't believe it could happen to me, happen here. Even with my parents teaching me how shit was, I still thought *that* kind of devastation happened somewhere else. It was that level of suffering, of realizing any suffering can happen to any of us if we allow it to happen to others. I think that has really informed my magic. Not intentionally, like my magic didn't come from thinking. I just was suffering so much. And I'd have these impulses to do something to relieve the despair, to move something, to move my mother's bones down to my father's model. And . . . you know how when you're sleeping wrong, your body will adjust, and you don't wake up? For a while it was like that. I was adjusting, getting comfortable, but not awake in it . . . but also like becoming faithful to this way of being before I knew my old ways weren't enough."

Ajana's eyes were soft. Dune had never shared her experience of H-8 before Murmur City with anyone but Dawud and Rio. But she figured Mama Rue knew from their mergers. It was stark to say it aloud and feel more known. And to know that soon she would hold more of Ajana's story. She was already so glad she was doing this project.

The third card was the Hermit, a solitary figure with a lantern heading into the darkness.

Dune didn't even need the question for this one. "Oh yeah, the Hermit is my card. I think my magic emerged because of the depth of my solitude. I was preparing myself for being alone forever." Dune chuckled bitterly. "Before I found Dawud, I wasn't sure if I wanted to make it another winter. But in that solitude I started to sense, feel, glimpse another world. Another way. Inside me, in the windows, in the trees—there's so much more life in everything than I understood before. Under the noise, under the decay, under the sadness, it's just life, a little green growth on everything."

Ajana was smiling now, mysterious. She turned over the fourth card, the Magician. They both laughed. Ajana asked, "Do you believe in magic?"

"Not really, even now. I am a linear thinker, so when my magic happens I am always surprised because it's never the expected next step. It's like I'm walking backwards. There's déjà vu, like I know I did it and I know why it was needed."

Ajana interrupted, "Why was the wall needed?"

"*You* know."

"Tell me again."

"Because H-8 was intentional. And the people who did that to us, who slaughtered us in our homes without a drop of blood spilt, they were coming to claim Detroit as the spoils, as their white utopia. And . . . the city does not want that."

"The city?" Ajana's tone was light, but her eyes were heavy.

"And me. I thought we were all here for the duration. I thought we were all taking this *stand*. It felt collective. My magic always feels like . . . a lot of people need it, make it root and grow."

Ajana nodded.

"And it gave us a chance, it gives us a chance to practice something. I watched my parents have all the best ideas about how we could move forward, about how humans could be with each other, but we were always under one attack or another. There was always a distraction and something else to handle. They never got a chance to just see what was possible, how far we could grow. So . . . yeah. I believe in experimentation. I believe in time and what we can do if given the time. And I feel so safe here. I have never in my life felt like I could be home outside my house."

Ajana turned over the final card. It was the Ten of Cups. The card of joy and love.

Dune started crying, surprising herself. She tried to stop, tried to pull herself together and answer. She couldn't. She couldn't even begin to explain what was coming up inside of her, both ecstatic joy and an anticipatory grief that snatched her breath from her throat. Ajana moved close, placing a hand on Dune's knee. Through her tears, Dune recognized the move as one that Berta sometimes did when the emotions were big. She wondered if Ajana was apprenticing with Berta, or if something in her knew this was a comfort that would work for Dune. The thought that all this safety and comfort could be gone, and soon, overwhelmed her again. And she wept for Maroon Detroit, and Ajana stayed until she was done crying. And Dune didn't try to explain. And she forgot to stop the recording until Ajana had gone.

Dune was grateful to learn something important—to be asked about one's gifts is tender. Our gifts are tied to our survival, and our survival is often rooted in our loss. And Dune had lost enough for three lifetimes.

Dawud

"Who am I in today's shenanigans?" Dune's voice matched her hand, moving along Dawud's belly in a spiral of the exact pressure he could handle without feeling either ticklish or bruised. Her tolerance for pain and pressure was much higher than his.

"Heartless wench."

"No sting."

"Venomous hag."

"Ooh, I felt that—and what, pray tell, is my offense?"

"You are determined to break your heart on me. Smash it straight into me. And—"

"Bad form old chap." Dune's voice was cold despite the humor. He was breaking *her* heart, after all.

"Sorry. It just feels unfair." They were both quiet for a moment. She wasn't going to ask for more, but he had more to say. "You're making it about you again. About us. I haven't done that to you. When you were slippery over Rio I didn't take it personally. When you wanted to leave our perfectly fine, if slightly overgrown house for this liberated *carpeted, sterile, canned-air* office monstrosity, I came with you. I love you. I even survived a pandemic for you."

Dune curled into his arm and spoke against his chest, "So why do you need to go now?"

"I never said I *need* to go," Dawud paused, Dune's face popped up to fact check his memory. "Ok, maybe I said it. But what I meant is I need to *be able* to go. Go or stay, I need it to be my choice. I will probably choose to stay, but—"

"*Probably* is such a stressful word in this context." She was mumbling into his shoulder, but he understood.

"We honest with each other, right?"

"Aren't you supposed to be honest *and* kind? *And* necessary?"

He made this little harumph sound and put a hand on her back, taking the other hand in his, swaying her a bit in a horizontal dance with him. "Nothing I am saying is unkind, baby. It is honest and necessary. To me anyway. I want you to know what I feel. I love you to fucking tiny supernova pieces."

Dune rested her head again. And she heard him. It flooded through her—he wasn't running from her. He just had to be able to run. She could be hurt all day if she wanted to, but she had no reason to be angry. As the truth moved through her it found all the parts of her coiled around that anger.

He started telling her about the next guest he was bringing on his show, a botanist who wanted to report on the re-emergence of endangered and extinct species in Maroon Detroit. "Speaking of magic," he said, and she understood. Dawud began listing out the names he liked: "Regal fritillary. Mitchell's satyr. Those are butterflies I think, or moths? Lark sparrows are back, and piping plover. Birds. Someone pulled a blue pike out the river the other day, catch and release . . ." She kept softening in his arms until he was really able to hold her.

The Magics

Dune set up the Magic Map space in Wind Tower, a large room with three small offices off of it, all facing north toward the city. Dune picked the coziest, darkest room as the interview room. It held an end table and two folding chairs, two microphones on boom stands, hooked up to a Zoom H5 recorder Dawud had given her. The other two small rooms weren't in use yet, but she had dragged a mattress into one of them in case she needed a nap.

The main space was the outline of an immersive map. She had marked the outer edges of Detroit and used painter's tape to show the main thoroughfares. She had pushpins and index cards, and was going to track her data using a system like the Detroit model her father had set up in their basement. Her plan was to map where people had lived in the city before H-8 because she was interested in the different kinds of magic that might exist in relation to specific neighborhoods, histories, grocery stores, proximity to the river. What made H-8 change some people's minds, and other's spirits? She felt nerdy and excited.

With the council's help, Dune hung flyers up all over Murmur City, as well as secure contact boxes where people could put their name in for an interview. Today she had three scheduled, each an hour long, with time in-between. She laid her wand on the interview table, making the process sacred. The first interviewee to enter the space was a young brown-skinned man named Yazan. He glanced around.

Dune's list of questions was simple: describe your magic, when did you first notice it, and is it still active?

"That old lady you roll with, she said I'm a shifter," he started. "Since H-8. Everyone treats me so good, like somehow, I bring them peace. Your grandma or whatever, she saw me, she said I was shifting for each person, like only *they* saw what they saw. I don't know what they see. Occasionally I'll catch my hands changing, mostly I don't feel it. It's not drastic, it happens as they look at me. Right now, I am one of the most beautiful people you've ever seen, right?"

Dune was stunned to realize how right he was. She'd been thinking he might be related to Rio. She laughed at this observation and touched the wand, which helped her recover. She returned to her list of questions.

"In the mirror I always look like me."

She arched a brow.

"Ok. The best version of me—the smoothest, sharpest, clearest-eyed version of me. The best of me, the selfie I send my honey and put on my profile. I have to be careful; I could get away with ... anything."

His eyes changed, looking directly into hers. Looking at him this way, softening her gaze, she thought she could see a peripheral version of him that was very different from what her eyes showed her.

"I have no idea who I am anymore. I please everyone. I keep pushing, trying to find an edge. I need to find a use for this."

"You survive because everyone you meet can feel safe around you." Dune still had one hand on her wand. She reached her other hand forward and softly touched Yazan's face. He looked surprised, and in the surprise his face shuddered before her. "Do you feel that?" She asked in a whisper. He nodded. "That's you."

His face went limp in her palm, somewhere between relief and exhaustion. Something was pouring from him, and Dune felt a certainty in her, that she was channeling, that the wand was helping, and that whatever this comfort and clarity was, it was part of her purpose now.

Dog Notices

Outside is changing. Down in the cold earth, something is pulling life in tight.

Outside is pressing in, the smells all getting closer.

I have to find a way to tell the people.

Part 4

Spring, Create

Closing In

Berta on the Isle

Berta's invitation was simple, "Come to the Isle."

Dune hadn't seen Berta in a while, hadn't felt the need. But she never knew she needed help until it was too late. Given all that was coming up with the wall, it would certainly help to spend some time with her healer. The weather was turning towards the bright, sunny, cool patterns of spring, so Dune decided to bike the five miles. Dog was elated to run alongside her. It felt so good to push her legs, to cut against the wind, her mobility increasing with the temperature. She zigzagged some on Jefferson Avenue, because she could.

In front of the Belle Isle Bridge was a sign in many languages. Near the bottom she found English: "We reclaim Wahnabezee. Invitation Only."

Three aunties sat on folding chairs on the bridge, talking. They weren't blocking the entrance, but it was clear she needed to check in with them before crossing. She introduced herself, saying her name, her parents' names, and that she was born in Detroit and now lived in Murmur City. She shared that Berta had invited her. The eldest woman pulled a walkie talkie out from the folds of her skirt and spoke into it in a language Dune couldn't understand. The elder listened intently to a long answer and then smiled at Dune with raised eyebrows, waving her past.

Dune had grown up spending summers on the island, but hadn't been back since H-8. From the long bridge that reached across this side of the Detroit River, she could see the beauty of the wall in a different way, the way the waves moved under and against it. It felt so close. She could see how it curved as it went west, turning to move across the land. It was so stunning to her, a wonder of the world that had, in some way, emerged from her being.

Berta had told her to turn right when she got across the bridge and there was a slight downhill slope to the turn, which meant she flew onto the island. There were new structures everywhere; an Anishinaabe village built in and around the state park buildings, abandoned zoo, and botanical garden. Dune rode until she saw Berta, watching for her, sitting on the grass that faced the city. Berta looked younger and more enthusiastic than she did in their healing sessions. Dune propped her bike up on its stand and hugged the healer.

"Dune, you look like a new person!" Berta exclaimed, taking her in thoroughly.

Dune laughed, "Thanks to you. You really helped me get out of bed and into my skin."

"You did the hard work. Grief is like having an iceberg land squarely in your heart. Only way through is to let it melt, to flood, pour it back out of you."

"Ah, that's what it was." Dune felt a bit embarrassed to remember ways Berta had seen her. "It's beautiful, what y'all have built here."

Berta turned and surveyed her home, her village. She looked back at Dune and shrugged, "It's been a different kind of chaos here. All humans are human. Anyway, I wanted you to meet some people."

Berta led Dune to a circle of people sitting near a small tree, not much taller than her. She recognized Sharon, but the other three—another woman and two men—she didn't know. As Berta introduced them, Dune understood that this was what was left of her healer's family. The older man, who Berta had called Uncle, was looking at her with deep familiarity.

"Did we meet? Before?" Dune asked him.

"Yes, many times, when you were very little. Your dad, Brendon, he and I did some organizing together. He was like me," Uncle tapped his chest with gorgeous hands, well used. "History buffs. I taught him about this place, how precious it is. I came to your house every day one summer, to help him set up a model of this Bending River city in his old basement," Uncle laughed, remembering. "You were shorter then."

Dune laughed with him, pulling for the memories, finding stills where she wanted film. Summers were spent outside when she was little. But it was ok, as long as one of them remembered.

"Anyway, Berta thought it was time we reconnected. And that you got to meet this tree." He leaned over and placed one hand against the young trunk. "This is Kama's tree."

Dune's breath caught. "What do you mean?"

"We loved your parents. When Brendon died, we all came. Your mother had her own rituals to honor him, and she let us be a part of those. As organizers, as warriors, we respected her. When we found out she had died, and there was no ritual for the people to tend to her spirit, we planted this tree for her. We made sacrifices to help her spirit on her journey. It's a Swamp White Oak, sturdy, humble, lives a few hundred years."

Matching her Uncle's light tone, Berta added, "We wanted you here, but we didn't know if you would ever leave the house. Then life got to falling apart. And I realized last time I held you that maybe you didn't even know she was here. And every time I touch this tree, she calls for you."

Dune stepped closer to the tree, with curiosity.

"Take your time. We'll be over there." Berta pointed down the way to a structure that had cloth walls rolled up on the sides. They drifted away, unhurried, talking amongst themselves, Dog in their number. Uncle had a mischievous look to him, and she knew they would sit together again.

Once they were well away, Dune stepped closer to the tree, wondering if she would feel Kama's presence here. She had been journaling ancestral thoughts for months and though they'd been more collective each entry, she still felt the distinct imprint of her mother. The origin tree of the wall had indicated her mother was everywhere—could she be here *and* everywhere?

Dune's hands reached for the tree. Her heart reached for the tree. She leaned against it and let herself rest.

Movement

Dune found Berta after she'd sat with her mothertree for a long time. Not only did she feel Kama, she sang to her. She had pressed her wand against the slender trunk of the tree, wanting Kama to know she was somehow a tree person too. She felt how much life was in this small tree, how long it was going to live.

She approached her healer and friend with huge gratitude to offer, but Berta's energy was so drastically shifted that Dune put a hand on her healer's arm and asked if she was ok. Berta's eyes looked sad and unsettled.

"Something's happening with the wall, Dune. Did you know?" Berta's voice was tentative, as if there was more to her question.

Dune frowned her no. "Something like what?"

"It seems to be moving. Not by a lot, but enough that our fisher people noticed it today—some of their best fishing spots are now . . . outside."

Dune felt a little nauseous. Had she done something awful? She tried to mask her worry, her guilt. "I will figure out what's happening, Berta, I promise."

Dune turned to leave and then doubled back, kneeling in front of Berta, lowering her head. "Thank you so much for showing me my mother's tree. Please thank everyone who helped to plant and care for it. And let me know how I can help care for it in the future."

Berta's hand touched Dune's head gently, "You are always welcome here."

Dune rode home double speed. She needed to ask Mama Rue for guidance.

Mama Rue

Dune felt the distinction between Rue and Mama Rue as she searched. She needed the guide, not the woman. She'd gone to her teacher's quarters, the dining room, and the fish gardens first, attempting to appear calm for any possible witnesses. She finally found Mama Rue in the Code Midnight Reading Room, sitting by herself in one of the round booths.

Her head was wrapped in white. She had likely been in ceremony and was here for respite. Her eyes were closed, and Dune noticed how otherworldly her face looked, ancient and eternal and lit from within. Her outfit was a lot of things that didn't go together in any obvious way—a vest woven with parrots and palm trees over a long-sleeved tie-dyed shirt, a bright yellow leather pencil skirt over purple joggers, and two different colored sneakers. Dune approached quietly, hoping the meditation was almost over.

"What." Mama Rue opened her eyes, squinting at Dune.

Dune shared what she had heard from Berta.

Mama Rue started laughing and did so for some time, so hard she was waving a hand and trying to catch her breath. Dune had time to feel frustrated and then hurt, and then recognize it *was* a little funny to be surprised by the behaviors of a magical wall. Eventually, she felt wide enough to hold both Berta's fear and her own, and Mama Rue's amusement. Only then did Mama Rue's laughter quiet.

"First of all, every time you say it's a wall, I cringe. It's never been a wall. It's always been a portal, between the past and the future—it's always been a medicinal vine, a relation. It's always been here to help us. It's always been alive. It's always been at choice, and you've never been in charge. You've been an inspiration, a liaison. You've been a point of entry; you've been a channel."

"But everyone thinks I am in some control of it. And . . . it did come because of me."

"It's confusing to be a channel. So much beauty and brilliance flow through you and you can't take it personally, not think it's you personally. Your brilliance is in being clear enough to channel—there is something impossibly pure in you, yes, but the wisdom comes before and beyond you."

"So . . . are you saying the past is closing in on the future?"

"On the outside of this portal, there are millions and millions and millions of people still caught in the past, caught in a past where their ancestors can't hear them, and they can't hear their ancestors. Where death is an end, where they live a life without spiritual companionship. Where they live a life completely disconnected from the Earth. Where they live a life trying to dominate each other and the Earth."

"So how do I protect all that's in here?"

"One second—do you have some magic on you?" Mama Rue frowned, looking Dune up and down. Dune pulled the wand from her pants. Mama Rue held it as she spoke, "In here is the only way *we* survive on this planet, for however long it exists. In here *we* partner with our ancestors and know death is a new assignment. In here, *we* walk with spirit as an additional limb, as a part of our internal and collective ecosystem. In here we gratefully receive everything that Earth wants to offer us, from wisdom to food. In here, we understand that power is always moving between us, and the work is to share it, understand it, and use that power to protect each other and the Earth. Here it's Black as fuck, it's Detroit as fuck, it's sustainable as fuck. But humans never know how lucky we are."

Dune waited, watching Mama Rue's grip tighten on the wand as she moved through her thoughts. She always spoke like she was just coming across the thought for the first time, but also already knew it was true.

"The good news is that this is what the rest of the country has to look forward to, this is what the rest of the world has to look forward to. The grief is coming to everyone, irresistible for real, an inevitable wave of overwhelming grief for having to lose so much all at once. For some, it will come in a virus made by man. For some, it will come in a crisis made by man. But it will come. There is no natural disaster that produces the kind of grief we faced here, grief imbued with rage at the injustice of it all, at the targeting of it all. The grief you feel when the drones bomb your village, when a sniper shoots and kills your child—it's so different from the grief you feel when your child dies in a flood, an earthquake." Mama Rue's eyes were distant; she was looking at memory again. "The earthquake was simply the Earth's process, an Earthly adjustment, no intention of harm. The sniper . . . That means someone looked at your child and decided that his life was worth less than a a bullet, and could be taken. Could be stolen. Could be collateral damage."

Mama Rue looked up at Dune, and Dune could see that so many children had been taken from her.

"And we have generations upon generations of unjust death amongst us all. So here, as we have done in the past, we have stolen ourselves away into maroon space. And I know some of your people, your council, have been in a real tizzy about a multiracial or multicultural maroon space. Let me tell you something, it was always this way! Black people were not a people when we came here. We were a small, dark, united nations trying to understand each other enough to say *freedom*. We were multitribal on the plantation, we made Blackness over a long period of being forced to share space and escape it. And when we crept into the swamps, other peoples awaited us. Sometimes a people that might look a lot like us, dark as the sun when you stare at it. Or sometimes different, hair long and thick where we were wooly and round. Or might just be someone from a different family in our same people. But it used to be that a different family, a different tribe meant a different culture. It was always different cultures coming together in the swamp, in the places no one wanted to live. And it was always making those places into pockets of life and freedom—that's what we've always done, that's how we've always survived apocalypse. We never had a wall; we always had a place that you couldn't find if you didn't know how to see it. Those vines, those willows weeping, that moss, all that soft, thick curtain. We always had a way of blending into the colors of earth, not being above the mud."

Dune felt restless. "But what do I *do*?"

Mama Rue pressed the wand into Dune's hands. "There's nothing *to do*. Just be. I mean it! Look, I know you want an *answer* and all I can offer you is a direction. Don't diminish your magic into a border wall. You opened a maroon portal. It came into existence from *our* needs, from *your* discipline to your magic. That means it is malleable, it is in relationship to you and to us. And maybe you know how to make more."

Dune's Ancestor Journal, March
Dune tried to see if her ancestors had some insight.

how long did you think we were going to stay in here?
forever? no container is forever. forever?
ok sure, but even forever isn't one thing, but many. we hope your forever outlasts ours, but age is only a factor of forever for those old enough to wonder if they really want to keep going. some of us don't

get that far, we die without leaving the present. some of us die just as we realize we want more time. some of us get sick so the time we have feels like forever, and some of us get sick in ways that make us wish we had forever more days with our beloveds.

tell somebody what you need.

you know—help.

Mbongi Council

The next day there was an Mbongi Council meeting and Dune got there ahead of anyone else, with Dawud as her support. She scribbled her name on the whiteboard's agenda with the word URGENT.

When Hoka arrived she beelined for Dune. "Are you ok?"

"Yes, but I need the council's help. The wall is shrinking." Dune tried to sound matter of fact, but there was still a tremor there.

Hoka didn't look surprised until she saw the look on Dune and Dawud's faces. "Well, of course, we're tracking the perimeter!"

Dune was stumped. "And?"

"And it's getting smaller." Hoka shrugged with open hands. "I'm glad you're back, kid."

As Hoka called the meeting to attention, Dune scanned the faces in the room, feeling silly and late. She couldn't shake the feeling that the wall closing in might be her fault, her weakness.

After Hoka and Mama Tazina had reviewed the agenda, they moved into a conversation about the wall. First Mohamed asked Dune how she had known about the change. Dune explained that the Anishinaabe fisherman saw it and that it was already impacting them. Then it was her turn to speak.

"Hoka said you're tracking the perimeter? Tracking how?"

Mohamed nodded at this question, expecting it and eager to answer. "Well, as we mentioned to you some weeks ago, we have been wanting to understand more about the wall. Initially my cartographer, Tomas, and I did just a very simple measured drive around the city, as close as we could get, which was a bit faulty and indirect but gave us a sense that we were in a roughly eight-mile circumference." Mohamed seemed amused, "I mean, it doesn't hurt that the wall ran along Eight Mile and Southfield."

Dune didn't laugh. Neither did anyone else.

"Ok. So, we used a drone to get some overhead shots, just for more reliable data. We can only get about six thousand feet up, and the drones drop from the sky if we get closer than two miles to the wall. Last week, Tomas went out to just check on the boundary and the wall was closer, on the inside of Southfield Road, and the south side of Eight Mile. Seemed like maybe a fluke or just a seasonal thing, but yesterday the drone showed a loss of nearly a mile all around. We drove out and barely made it past Seven Mile."

Dune's stomach tremored. "Was anyone hurt?" Killed?

"Not to our knowledge. Since the wall . . . appeared, we have really encouraged people to stay at least a mile from it. We have lost some farmland."

Dune was grateful. She couldn't handle it if people had died because of something she should have told them about—though she hadn't known, only felt, plus what could she have said? Her stomach rolled.

"We can't tell yet if the wall is getting thicker—if the wall is becoming more of a forest, or if the total circumference is just . . . closing in."

Looks passed around the table and landed back on Dune.

"So you didn't... know?"

Dune shook her head no, mouth too dry to speak.

"You didn't move some stuff around in your magic model?" Ed, the closest thing she had to a nemesis, asked his question as if it were the obvious cause. Dawud bristled next to her.

Dune cut Ed with her eyes, and cleared her throat. "If the wall is getting thicker, it could be to protect us. If it's moving . . . it could mean . . ."

"We are all gonna die?" Ed chuckled nervously and Dune felt an unfamiliar wave of compassion for him. Everyone here was just as scared as she was, even if they each showed it differently.

"We have to adapt again," Mama Tazina offered. Dune nodded with gratitude.

"Well, I came here looking for help because I don't know if this can be fixed, but I know I can't do this alone." Dune looked at Hoka as she spoke, trying to borrow some calm from her leadership. Hoka nodded, but her mind was clearly elsewhere.

Ajana spoke up, "I'll help you, Dune. I think we need to come up with two kinds of solutions. I think you and I should go out and communicate with the wall, the plants in the city, see what we can learn and hear. And I think we need to gather some information on other options—are there places where the wall seems thinner? Do we know what's happening under the water in the river? Is there a way to make an opening?"

"No offense, but you don't think the US military has already checked all of that out?" Ed's voice was deflated. Ajana shook her head.

"Of course, but they're outside. The wall came from us, came from one of us with a need and some magic. Doors lock in different ways. They lock out and they lock in. Just because a door is locked doesn't mean the person inside is locked in. Do you know what I mean?"

"I do," Dune answered. "This was definitely meant to lock people out; it grew around us to protect us. And it's not coming down, but coming in. That must be significant."

Mohamed spread his fingers out on the table. "We have to consider that we might be under attack."

"We have to consider everything and then figure out what we can actually do," Hoka affirmed. "Ajana is right. Mohamed is too. Mo, will you lead a team to do another round of checking for weaknesses and openings in the wall? And Dune, Ajana, will you come with me to talk to the wall?"

Dune felt the urge to tell them about the chorus singing in the tree, in her wand. She overrode it—it felt unserious, inappropriate. She couldn't find the words, much less say them. "Let's go."

A Little Magic

"I don't understand. I thought the wall was here to protect us." Ajana sounded so young. They were all piled into the flaming truck Dawud had claimed as his favorite.

"It has," Hoka was so gentle and matter of fact. Dune appreciated how Hoka always reminded everyone she spoke to that life is not an either/or paradigm, but a multi-truth practice ground.

"Why do you think it's changing?" Dune asked, Dawud's fingers drumming nervously against her thigh. Dune was pressed between Dawud and Hoka in the rarely used middle front seat.

"Hmmm. Honestly . . ." Hoka was watching Dune's face, the way Kama used to watch her piece together a new word. "Sometimes it helps me to consider the opposite—why did the wall come, why has it stayed? Maybe the wall was just to give us a chance. To practice utopia, practice togetherness, without all the distraction. Maybe we have outgrown it."

Hoka sounded doubtful and Dune leaned into the inquiry, "But how does the wall know we're *ready*? We are barely getting it all going now. It works, but maybe it only works like this. Maybe it only works without all the people and shit out there."

"Maybe. But no one gets to escape, cherie," Bineshii spoke up from the backseat. "My people have tried so many times, to just live right with the Earth in smaller and smaller pockets. So far, the world crashes in every time. That's the truth of being human, the cost of it. We are bound up with each other, even the misguided ones. We are one Earth, all in relationship to each other no matter how much we fortify our barriers. We never have been one little pocket of safe space surviving despite the planetary downfall—the river still flows, the sun still shines, our loved ones are everywhere—we are of the world. And we have years! To take one of the most devastating things to happen in history and turn it into peace, interdependence, life."

Dune felt a primal longing for everything to stay the same. Dawud asked, "Do we die in here?"

"No. I don't think so," Hoka said, truly looking thoughtful. "But we may need a way out. And I suspect we're the ones who will find it."

Dune felt exhausted, as if she could anticipate the weight of the machete in her hands. And then she heard a voice from within, the voice of her journals—

no silly. like jonah. like harriet. like siddhartha. like eshu. like lilith. like you invited us, love. grief. magic. we will help you. everyone in here has a little magic.

Grace

They drove up Jefferson until they were about a quarter mile from the wall, which loomed across the whole world at this distance. The wind seemed to blow all around them, constant, making a soft rustling music with the leaves. They approached quietly, Hoka, Dawud, and Bineshii falling a few steps behind Ajana and Dune, but staying close. When they reached the wall, Dune felt a pull, like she wanted to fold into the leaves and rest, and it wanted to hold her.

Ajana placed her hands against the wall, which suddenly seemed incredibly vibrant and active, as if she was sunlight and it needed her. She closed her eyes, her breath slowing down as she began to listen. Dune had only seen her do this twice. Each time it felt like she was being given the most exquisite gift, watching the translation of sunlight into story.

"They aren't . . . mad at us. They were waiting for you Dune." Ajana was listening as she spoke, her eyes moving behind the lids.

"What should we call them?" Dune suddenly knew that *they* was the living entity in front of them. This had eluded her—this wasn't just a wall, it wasn't just a portal. This was a living creature.

"Grace." Ajana offered the name with no hesitation and all of them looked up at this green giant. "Aya Grace. Vine of grace. They say . . . *there can never be two worlds, even if one world has many concurrent times coexisting. there is one Earth, one world, all happening in one constant and forever now, which holds all that was and is and will be. each of us holds time together, we cannot be pulled apart.* Grace cannot do what is unnatural. Grace says, *we are one.* and, *whoever loves me can stay.*" Ajana giggled a bit, soft, the welcome pouring through her. "*Earth will grow anything we need, as long as we understand that everything will change, always, every time. Earth will heal from us, or with us. it's our choice, we must decide to be here."*

Ajana looked half elsewhere. Dune noticed the vines slowly wrapping themselves around Ajana's wrists, moving up her legs. Dawud stepped closer to Ajana, and Dune was unsure what he would do if the vines began to take the girl. Before he could touch her, Ajana started laughing. "Don't be afraid. They love us."

"Then why is it shrinking? Ask why," Hoka pressed the question, her voice hard even as her hand gently brushed against the broad leaves of Grace.

Ajana smiled now, "Oh! They thought that's what we wanted."

Glimpses

Detroit

Dune stepped up next to Ajana and placed her hands against Grace. As soon as she did, the vines whipped around her wrists. She felt smaller than she could remember, held thoroughly by hands as big as the sky. She didn't have Ajana's gift to see what was happening, but she could feel the protective clarity of the green creature flowing through her, through the city, forming the barrier. She could feel the multitudes of beings that made up Grace, spirits and ancestors. She could feel the life force of the city and, in that, she felt the vulnerability of the place, of the people.

Grace wouldn't leave them without protection.

Grace needed them to understand that *detroit wasn't ready to survive without protection*, and that *the whole Earth needed protection*, and *all the people who loved the earth needed protection* and that *Earth was a living entity, embodied in the earth, who wanted a relationship of mutual protection and care.*

They also knew Dune didn't want to enrage the people who wanted to leave. Dune felt how the desire to protect the people and place of Detroit was pulling Grace higher, and the desire to free people into their sovereignty was pulling Grace back into the dirt. It took effort to even comprehend this both-ways growing, and it occurred to Dune for the first time that this work could kill her. Maybe she wasn't up for this task. Without direction, she whispered, "What do I do?"

Feeling her feet on the tar of Jefferson Avenue, Dune was suddenly, simultaneously flying through a different Detroit—she could no longer see Grace. The river was wide all the way to the Canada side and the street beneath her was thick with life, filled with the bubbling play force of a festival. There were lots of people, wearing clothing that was ancient, colorful in a lot of different ways—traditional clothing of a multitude of peoples. There was dancing, there was food, and there was a Blackness penetrating every crowd, diverse as they were. She flew west, towards the Ambassador Bridge. The old highways were all reduced to wide two-way lanes that the people who needed vehicles used to get things around. The rest was green, fecund.

The stadiums were confusing to take in, so she dropped lower to understand. Ford Field was an incredible farm of raised beds! As she moved over the farmers, she heard one saying they might need to close the roof if the temperature dropped again.

She lifted up again, searching for something she couldn't quite name. She scanned the horizon, and in doing so realized that it was much broader than she'd seen in years. And Ajana was flying with her. She noticed Dune at the same moment, smiling in surprised and grateful recognition. They kept turning around until the wall—until *Grace* was visible, far, far away in the direction they'd come from, off to the east. They flew that way, along Jefferson, past Grosse Pointe, up where Lake St. Clair met Lake Huron. They flew until Grace filled their eyes.

That's when Dune saw an opening, at the base of the wall, as wide as the street. People were entering Grace's body from all around, but this was the only place Grace opened on the Maroon Detroit side.

Taking a moment to enjoy the sensation of her body in flight, Dune circled down. Ajana hovered in the air nearby. They watched people, one at a time, coming through the opening, and walking in. One person approached to enter Maroon Detroit—and Grace closed up, efficient, on the outside. People paused in place and looked away from the person, giving them the privacy of rejection, waiting for them to step back, turn around, and leave. Once they were out of sight Grace opened again, and the next person in line resumed crossing this holy border.

Dune understood, heart pounding, that people could come and go, but they had to be approved by Grace, by the city, by Earth itself. Those who left could always return, as long as they brought that peace energy to the Earth in this place.

A memory flashed through Dune's mind: she held Brendon's belt loops while he took photos of Kama standing at the gate to the old city of Fez in Morocco. To cross that gate was to enter a sacred city, a sacred place. Detroit was a sacred place in this vision. There was freedom, but it was rooted in reverence.

As the vision cleared, Dune could briefly feel herself both flying and standing, and then she was once again heavy and alert on a street she had always known, next to Ajana. And she understood so much.

Aya Grace had been born from the love of her parents, and the love of Dune and Dawud, and the love of Detroiters for each other and the land, and the love of the Anishinaabeg. And Grace had visions of their own.

Grace wasn't their first or only name. Grace was the force of life and healing that moved through everything. The great doctor, the healer, the builder, the protector, the mother and grandmother and great grandmother. And Grace had been ready to partner with Dune, but not just Dune. She wasn't the only one, or the first, anymore than Detroit was the first sacred space.

Dune received a word, a concept, a job—she was a doula of... boundaries? A doula of sacred space? No, a doula of a sacred future orientation. A future doula.

A future doula.

Slowly, as Grace let her go, Dune laid down and passed out.

Transmission

Dawud was holding her in a way he'd never held her before. She could hear his heartbeat, he was pressing her head against his chest, rocking her like she was a baby. Her limbs felt buttery, her joints melted. She didn't open her eyes, there was already so much information in all the sounds around her.

Dawud's heartbeat drummed under voices she loved, Hoka, Bineshii. Dog was here, circling her, protecting her, she could hear his breath. Ajana was breathing calmly, to her right. Jizo was here, holding her hand, she could tell. *Are you ok*, his hand asked hers, over and over again, childlike. Is she ok, give her room, she looks calm, she needs to rest, is she warm—the other voices sounded babbling-brook busy over the stones of Jizo's question and Dawud's heart.

I'm ok. She said it to Jizo, with her mind. Everyone went still, quiet. Maybe she had also said it aloud.

Dawud whispered against the top of her head, "Welcome back,

babe." And she could feel that he had been crying. She moved her left hand against the surface beneath her—asphalt, sun baked. Earth was also concerned for her. *I'm ok.*

Hoka's voice came next, clear. "Well, what happened?"

Dune wasn't sure her voice would work. She opened her mouth, feeling it was the first time she had even tried to use her face. She had to stretch a bit, opening her jaw and moving it around, contracting and yawning and playing with the soft meat of her cheeks. This took some time.

"It's not a wall. It's Grace—Aya Grace. Grace is our protector, the life in the dirt, in this place. Maybe everywhere." Dune played with opening her eyes and thought better of it. "When I cast the first spell that invited Aya Grace to grow into our border, I was just trying to protect us. And I didn't do it alone, it was all the spirits, the bones, the magic, the prayers of everyone who died. And everyone who loves the Earth, who was a part of me. We aren't safe without them, but they need our faith, our longing for their presence, to hold the ground, to hold us."

"Ah, so—that's why it's, she's been shrinking?" Hoka's voice was soft.

"They. That's why. But there's another way. Detroit can have a gate. We can have an opening, and anyone who loves the land is welcome. And anyone who doesn't won't get through until they heal their connection to the land. And we will grow. This can grow, here and anywhere people love the land. It's an ancient practice, making a space sacred. The original instruction is to recognize that each place is sacred. There are lots of us who can do this. I have some instructions now."

Ok, Kama said, on the same channel Jizo had used. *Rest now. That's enough for them and that's enough for you.*

Dune felt heavy as nightfall. She felt Dawud rocking her until the waves of grief and vision had washed her thoroughly. There was nothing else that needed saying.

Dog

The human who grew the city went flying from her body for a while, and she saw the best path ahead of us. The human who hears every green creature was flying too. The big green dog said hello to us.

Now I must help the humans, for they know nothing of sharing territory, and the alpha nature of everything green.

Recovery

Dune slept for most of the following week, waking up only to go to the bathroom, drink water, and eat. According to Rio, Ajana apparently had a long recovery period as well. Once the two of them were well, they would bring a detailed report of their vision and any rituals or instructions back to the council and community. Grace was growing again, and more and more people understood there was no wall, just a friend.

Dune sat in her recovery bed, looking out the window at Grace, who had receded all the way across the river. She felt into her magical capacity. There was a new system inside her body, which felt like both energy flowing in her nervous system and a new language tonguing at all her cells. She could talk to Earth in a way that invited this level of relational safety. This is one of the purposes that she was supposed to serve, to go to different places in crises, places that still have enough people who love them, and enough strong and present ancestors to create a stronghold there. She, Ajana, and others from Maroon Detroit were here to create this possibility of safe spaces, truly safe spaces in right relationship with the Earth.

This magic was only possible when all the people honored the land. The Earth had an inherent sense of generosity and equity. The size of each maroon enclave was set by the number of people within. The city had started shrinking because people wanted to leave, and it couldn't sustain the size of the city with so many people wanting something else! If more people came, the space would expand.

Dune had such a clear sense of her answer, not just to the questions of the wall, but every question she was asked.

Rio: Are you ready to return to my lovers' bed?
Dune: Yes.
Mama Rue: Are you done being my apprentice?
Dune: Yes and never.
Jizo: Can I just age like a normal person now?
Dune: Yes, but you will always be my little Jizo.
Dawud: Can we move out of here into a house?
Dune: Absolutely.

Dune could feel her life path ahead of her, calling. She and Ajana would learn how to communicate what they knew. Maybe one day they would teach others to do this spell, creating pockets of land where only the people who loved it could root there. This was a land back spell! It was never just about protecting these people, but about returning land back to those who loved it, and returning the people to abundant Earth. The Anishinaabe had taught Brendan to love Detroit, and his and Kama's love had been foundational in starting the spell. Brendon loved Detroit, he loved the place of Detroit, coming and going, how it changed, what it held—he loved everything to do with Detroit. Love for Detroit was in Kama's bones. They had grown Dune inside that love, which is why she had never considered leaving. Her love with Dawud, her romance with Rio, her family with Jizo and Captain and Dog and this city, infused the dirt . . . She belonged to Detroit, she loved the land.

And in this way, the land of Maroon Detroit is growing still.

A Way

River Ritual

The majority of Detroit survivors gathered on the beach of Wahnabezee as the wind wrapped itself around each of them, lifting the light cloth off their bodies and then back against them, tight. Everyone wore whatever they had that was closest to white. Elders led the way, walking slowly, with baskets of fresh herbs from the first spring harvest.

Bineshii had organized this sunrise ritual when Dune had asked for help. Dune had a song that she thought was meant to open the portal, but couldn't see the rest of the ritual. Bineshii guided each person to offer and anoint—first, to pick an herb from the basket and offer it into the small waves of the river. Then, she dipped her hand in the water and anointed the person behind her, Mama Tazina, looking at the crowd, *like so*. Now the shoreline was busy with blessings, anointings, and offers.

Dune lingered at the back of the crowd, amazed at how big the community was around her. There was even a circle from the

Cave—Kat, Roush, and Lucinda stood in gray robes, helping their friends in and out of the water. Mohamed stood a bit farther down the beach, surrounded by people Dune could barely see, his people, there and not there. She understood the risk they were taking, to be part of this community, and she understood there were hundreds of them, obscured but alive. Dune gripped her wand, nervous to sing in front of this many people, hopeful that the nerves would pass when it was time.

When her bare feet touched the cold water, Dune felt like the river was pulling her in and down. She closed her eyes, feeling the spirits in the glacier and snow that fed the lake that fed this river. Mama Rue walked up next to Dune, and without much fanfare, dipped her hand in the water, brushing her river-doused thumb up over Dune's brow. Dune returned the prayer, anointing her teacher. Since meeting Grace, Dune could feel that Mama Rue would only be her teacher now, for the duration. With the blessing of the river, Dune felt strength flow through her body, eradicating the black hole of hunger. She wasn't afraid; love was on either side of the river, above and below the surface.

Dune stepped out of the water, turning towards the women leading the ceremony. Bineshii nodded to Dune, who took in a breath. Suddenly, she was singing one note of loss, her head thrown back in the wailing of a grief the size of a city, the size of an era, the size of a history, the size of a people, the size of a future. The wound that had claimed Dune's mother was healing into a portal through which Black people found a different way of being, a way of living in safety. A place beyond life or death, a place of peace, a place stolen from time and space. The wound was closing now, the Earth and the people stitching back together.

Then Dune, wand in her left hand like a conductor, began to sing alone,

> Open the way inside you
> The universe is your only breath
> Surrender to the present moment
> Don't hurry in your dance with death
> Turn towards your life,
> What's coming now is all that's left

And Mama Rue sang back to her, "What's coming now is all that's left." Mama Rue took her hand, and Dune felt the song flow through them. Together they sang a song they had never heard before.

> Many rivers flow through us
> Many creatures become us
> Many storms change the journey
> The dirt keeps calling us home
>
> Open the way inside you
> The universe is your only breath
> Surrender to the present moment
> Don't hurry in your dance with death
> Turn towards your life
> What's coming now is all that's left
> What's coming now is all that's left
>
> Seed the soil within you
> You drumbeat! You shimmering leaf
> Listen for the sound of sunlight

> Live a life that's worth your grief
> Turn towards your life
> What's coming now is all that's left,

Dune sang alone: "What's coming now is all that's left," knowing her body was precious, knowing her life was her own, knowing that there would be a way to leave the city when the time came and it would be easy. She was free. They were free.

Mama Rue sang back, "What's coming now is all that's left," knowing that she could be mad, loved, and useful. She was free.

And the people around them started singing it, "What's coming now is all that's left." Dune felt the wand come alive in her hand and she raised it up. The wand moved gently, and she let it guide the crowd into choir. Steadfast as a metronome, the wand helped the song click into each body, into its timeline in history. Held by the breath, they all felt the freedom of survivors, of being able to decide for themselves how to move into the future—as a crisis, as a possibility, as a home. They sang it, over and over, until the water took the song away on the waves.

Marta Comes Home

Marta wasn't the first person through the portal, but she was in the first cluster of people to see an opening. To say an opening is an exaggeration. What had seemed an impenetrable wall at one glance looked like an inviting path into a sunlit forest on the next. She could almost see all the way through. Others around her didn't react, but she saw two people in the distance stand up, gather their things and appear to walk into the wall. No one else seemed to notice. Marta understood that existing wasn't the end of the wall's magic.

She grabbed the bag she'd had ready since she arrived. She said nothing to the people camped near her because what was there to say? She sensed that if they were supposed to come through, they would. She walked up to the opening and was in it before she realized. As soon as she stepped into the green space she was in a different soundscape. Hushed, but with birdsong and a sound like people or water nearby, something moving faster than she was. She had a strong feeling of dual desires—she could have stayed in this wood without trees indefinitely, green soft and everywhere, mysteriously rising and falling and spacious enough for her to look around and see life everywhere. And she needed desperately to press on, to find Dune. To find Detroit.

Dune's Ancestor Journal, March

there was never just one detroit, and there isn't now. there is the million-projections collage of detroit from everyone beyond the city, and there are the roughly 800 experiences of the inhabitants who decided to stay and see what happened. there are those who were always trying to escape this city, and those trying to protect it, and those building it, and those resting in the container, waiting for the future. there is a future detroit as much as a pre and past detroit. there are Black people in every aspect of detroit's future. and there is the rich realm of ancestors, just a breath above you, just next to you. the places where the spirit realm touches and shapes the material and vice versa—those expand the city yet again into a multiverse.

there were plagues before this one—the plague is never the set of symptoms, never the virus. it is an exposure to the reality of our precarity, our predetermind independence. It is a way of seeing our care, or lack of care, in bright light. plagues compound each other, pressuring the norms of their time until we surrender, until we die or change. until we learn that life must be protected and danced towards. until we understand that nothing miraculous is promised. a plague can be a rescue operation for a people in hell and it can be a terror to those in the myth of heaven. beyond any plague is a question: do humans still want the gift of Earth? beyond this plague is the specific question: can Black people breathe and know peace on this Earth?

there is a small group of humans who are saying yes. more than one. this is the most hopeful thing we can tell you. another small group of humans, led by Indigenous and Black visionaries, have decided to belong to a place. and the place has accepted their stewardship, has chosen to protect them, has said yes to belonging to them. and it isn't a theoretical protection—it is a home that humans cannot enter without permission. there are many places like this on Earth, and you know of none of them unless you are invited.

a different small group of humans are flying and growing in every direction, dandelions blown, mycelium running, each holding the structure for surviving apocalypse and seeding a functional community within.

without new data to feed a ravenous media, detroit will become a ghost story to those beyond its border. with its small doses of magic, the residents of detroit will be able to make a way out of no way. when the world outside is as safe as the one within, perhaps, perhaps Grace will lay down from their reaching to the sun. perhaps, someday, we will let Earth hold us all.

Epilogue

Maroon Detroit-Waawiyaatinong Protocol

We are of this place. Our ancestors and our unborn and our future are the ecosystem of this place. We collaborate with seven generations of spirit to make every decision. We treat Earth like our skin, our blood, our breath, and our lives, because it is.

We begin by listening; we stay curious.

We let love lead.

Our boundaries allow us to love ourselves and each other.[1]

We are free to do anything that does not cause harm to, or limit the freedom of, another.

Whenever problems arise, we seek the insight and leadership of people already working on relevant solutions.

Whenever distrust arises, we seek connection or boundary without judgment.

---

1. Referencing the work of Prentis Hemphill, and the protocol itself honors both Indigenous land protocols and the Allied Media Conference principles.

We add to the wilderness. Help everything grow.

We generate our abundance, our longevity, and our safety, together.

The End/We Begin

The creek was moving slowly; the heat of summer made even the water languid. Dune straddled the wide log that served as a diving board over the creek, feeling strong from the swim and the climb. This swim spot had been a known secret through her childhood. Usually, one of her parents would bring her here while the other got some time to do the things adults did when their kids weren't around.

Back then Belle Isle would be a massive pulse of Black music from every era, pouring from car windows and open trunks, bodies in summer chic—fresh fades, new braids, short shorts, muscle tees, white kicks, pastel jellies, and sandals with endless straps that wrapped up around gleaming shaved legs. Her parent-of-the-day would wind their car through the crowds around the island to the northernmost parking lot, and then walk her towards the lighthouse until it was time to turn into the wooded path that would take them along the creek.

In her memory she could see Kama sitting on the shore, laughing with Elouise and other sisterfriends, very rarely touching the water, and even then only with her toes—Kama didn't swim and she was fine with that since she had neither gills nor fins. But she loved that young Dune was a fish in the water.

Dune's memory also showed her Brendon, his pant legs rolled up, bent over to examine the wildlife proliferating in the shallows. When she was little, Brendon was the one who took her into the water, who taught her to control her breath to make her body a flotation device. Who made her stand in the shallows amongst the river weeds until the feeling of what grew in the water didn't startle or disturb her. She remembered how strong and immortal he seemed then, a tree she could climb for safety.

Now she leaned forward, feeling the heat of the wood against her soft belly, resting her chin on her hands. The green wall was barely visible to the south, the sun high up above it, shining on them here. Bineshii had invited them to come visit Wahnabezee as much as they wanted, as long as they were respectful and left the Isle cleaner than they found it.

Dune's people were here, sprinkled amongst the Indigenous babies and teenagers, all flirting or play fighting in and out of the water. Dawud was across the creek on a blanket with Kat and Mohamed. Dune could tell by the speed of his hands moving through the air and the tapping motion in his feet and legs that he was excited about the idea he was sharing. And—was that a flirtatious glance between Dawud and Mohamed? She would hear about it later.

Dog stepped out of the creek and away from the lounging humans before shaking dry. He walked over and sat next to Dawud, tilting his head such that Dune suspected he was tuning fully into the conversation.

Jizo was in the water with most of the other kids. His hair was parted down the middle and dripping, his gorgeous teen smile graced with a bit of mustache now. She wondered how long this phase would last—days? Weeks? Months if they were lucky. He remained unimpressed by all the elders telling him to slow down, stay young, enjoy it. Hind was in the water too, her hair in ponytails. She and the other kids followed the quiet Jizo angel around, learning to communicate in his way, borrowing from his free and self-determined style.

She thought, "We never consider how precious time is until we realize ours, as we know it, will end." Then she let the thought drift away, as it might not even apply to her magical Jizo.

Marta was there on the beach, in a circle with Bineshii, Sharon, and Mama Tazina. Dune was taking it slow with Marta's miraculous return. The anger was long spent, forgiveness extended, and even though there was no romance left between them, friendship now felt . . . possible. No rush.

Rio was laying alone, a few humans down from Dawud. They wore a cropped muscle shirt and unzipped denim shorts, cut off and frayed at the knees. From here, her lover's hips looked like a shore. As was now their norm, as soon as Dune's attention touched them, Rio propped themselves up on an elbow and looked around as if called, found Dune's looking eyes, and smiled. Dune smiled back, noticing how sweet it felt to enjoy the connection without needing to hide—it was the same way she felt receiving warmth from the sun. Love from abundance. Dune felt Rio appreciating her thick thighs, the sun on her skin. She smiled, turning away, letting herself be worshiped.

Then her attention was pulled down to someone approaching in the water—Berta was stroking her way over with determination, moving like a mermaid between the splashing bodies at play; stealth under the peals of children's laughter. She pulled herself onto the rock next to Dune, squatting with ease and leaning forward, squeezing her long black hair until a small river flowed out and down the surface of the rock. Berta looked up at Dune with the darkest eyes, lines of joy beaming out into her skin, the only sign of age.

They had given themselves time, more time at their own pace, time to cherish and figure out life, time to love, time to find ways forward. They were in relationship to the Earth, to Aya Grace, to each other, and to their ancestors. Together, without speaking, they watched the sun dissipate the droplets. They had time.

Acknowledgments

This series is for every community that has been decimated by genocide, both those we know of and those that are only remembered by the Earth—may this story nourish our imagination of where and how all peoples continue. I offer deep bows of gratitude to my Detroit family, who taught me so much about community, commitment, place-based organizing, and transforming myself to transform the world. Thank you specifically to Sacramento Knoxx and Nick Reo for Anishinaabe and Ojibwe consultation to root the book in place. Thank you to my teachers, healers, Ayahuasca guides, ancestors, and spirit guides, who always remind me to imagine a future that all of us can opt into. And to AK Press and the Black Dawn Series, deep gratitude for trusting me with each book, and for giving me a place to learn to write long-form fiction.